T0161017

Endorsements

Jesus used stories that were simple to understand and packed with valuable lessons for life. JoAnn Vicknair has followed that model in her book, *It's Storytime, Memaw!* These short stories that she shared with her own grandchildren will bless your children and grandchildren as well.

Dr. Bill Skaar—Pastor, First Baptist Church, Grand Prairie, TX.

Teachers stress the educational importance of reading to children. *It's Storytime, Memaw!* contains captivating real-life stories that put God on the front burner of everyday life. A must for the home library.

Dick N. Walker—Retired Educator

As a pastor and as a father, I have always wanted my church and my children to see how the truth of the Bible can be applied to every step of life. JoAnn's stories have encouraged me because I see that she has done just that! Sharing memories like this in written form only enhances the impact of those who want to see God working in every area of life. Inspiring, indeed!

Pastor Adam Stanfield—First Baptist Church, LaPlace, LA.

As I read this book, I am amazed at how each story could influence a child's spiritual and moral thoughts and beliefs. At times, I found myself so interested in the stories, that I almost forgot that they were written for children. I highly endorse this book, not only for children, but for anyone who reads it and benefits from its Biblical teachings.

Diane Giardina—Retired Educator

As a Pastor and Father, these stories strike a vein that is desperately needed for this next generation, the art of storytelling. As a father of young children, I can attest that children are hungry for stories told to them, whether they come from scripture or about life in general. I highly recommend this book. *It's Storytime, Memaw!* provides rich material and integrates Bible truths that engage young minds.

Brandon Foottit—Minister of Students – First Baptist Church, LaPlace, LA

Sentimental and relatable to children and adults alike. God's fingerprint and love is evident in every word written in this amazing book!

CheraKee Epperly—VBS Director and Mother

As a grandmother and also an avid reader, JoAnn Vicknair's stories are delightful and refreshing to read. Her stories of fiction and non-fiction will be an encouragement and an inspiration to children of all ages.

Linda Neal—Active Sunday School Teacher, Retired Educator

These stories are true-to-life and heartfelt. I, as a pastor and father, especially appreciate the connection that so many make to the Bible and the Gospel. A great book to read along with a child or grandchild.

Rev. Shane Dismuke—Pastor First Baptist Church, Norco, LA

It's Storytime, Memaw! demonstrates JoAnn's love for the Lord and her desire for her grandchildren to know Jesus as their Savior. The stories are so personal, that I saw myself as a child in many of them. The illustrations are refreshing and children can easily understand and relate to each story. There is nothing more beautiful than a grandmother teaching her grandchildren about Jesus' love and acceptance and watching them grow up and mature in the Lord.

Kerry Charlton—Adult Sunday School Teacher and Grandmother

Some of my best memories as a child were my parents and grandparents telling me stories. JoAnn brings those joyful moments back to life in *It's Storytime, Memaw!* And I know God will speak to the listening hearts of children everywhere through these beautifully written treasures.

Sharon G.—Children's Sunday School Teacher

I am a grandmother and great-grandmother who loves to read stories to my grands. I love this book because it incorporates fascinating stories along with Godly principles for life. It is age appropriate for all, including grandmothers like me.

Ann Remondet—Administrative Assistant First Baptist Church

It's Storytime, Memaw! is a compilation of entertaining children's stories that provide a solid Biblical lesson. Children and adults alike will learn about God and the love He has for us in these Spirit-inspired stories!

Allison McDonald—Soon-to-be Grandmother

JoAnn's stories are perfect to read aloud. Accompanied by Bible verses, they lead children to ask questions and learn the life-lessons experienced by the characters. I can't wait to share them with my grandchildren.

Patty Cortez—Children's Ministry Team

JoAnn's stories are so entertaining to read to my grandchildren, and more importantly, their glory always goes to God! Even though the characters face a problem, they are directed to know where to go to seek God's Word. God placed these stories in JoAnn's heart and His truths shine through.

Gena S.—Grandmother

I love It's Storytime, Memaw! The stories bring back so many childhood memories. I'm thankful each story is followed up with Bible verses. I can't wait to read them to my granddaughters.

Connie McMillan—Grandmother

It's Storytime, Memaw!

An Answered Prayer for Stories That Point Children to God

JoAnn Vicknair

Carpenter's Son Publishing

Published by Carpenter's Son Publishing, Franklin, Tennessee

Published in association with Larry Carpenter of Christian Book Services, LLC
www.christianbookservices.com

Scripture quotations taken from the New American Standard Bible® (NASB), Copyright © 1960, 1962, 1963, 1968, 1971, 1972, 1973, 1975, 1977, 1995 by The Lockman Foundation. Used by permission. www.Lockman.org

Scripture is used from the The Holy Bible, Today's New International Version® unless otherwise noted. Copyright © 2001, 2005 by Biblica®. Used by permission of Biblica®. All rights reserved worldwide.

Scripture quotations marked NKJV are taken from the New King James Version of the Bible, copyright ©1982 by Thomas Nelson, Inc. Used by permission.

Scripture quotations marked (ESV) are from the ESV® Bible (The Holy Bible, English Standard Version®), copyright © 2001 by Crossway, a publishing ministry of Good News Publishers. Used by permission. All rights reserved. Scriptures marked KJV are taken from the KING JAMES VERSION (KJV), public domain.

Edited by Christy Callahan

Cover Design and Interior Layout Design by Suzanne Lawing

Interior images by Jamie Hornberger of j. louise creations

Printed in the United States of America

978-1-952025-19-8

Dedication

Who heard my prayer for children's stories that would glorify God? God did. Who knew God would choose me to publish stories He gave me? God did.

Who knew regardless of spiritual warfare, that through Him, I would succeed? God did. And God knew this before He created me. Hallelujah! I was created for this.

I insist all the praise and glory go to God, for these are His stories given to me about many of my life's actual events, to share with you. Your children will be compelled to see God in their everyday lives because He is in *everything*. God is in the good, the sad, the heartache, the joy, the anger—everything!

Open the box. Let God out. He created the universe. He gives strength to the weak and power to the powerless. I am living proof. Praise God!

Contents

* denotes a true story

Acknowledgments

I praise God Almighty for choosing me to write and publish His stories to draw children and adults alike, closer to Himself.

I thank my husband, Phillip, for his unconditional love and support during this whirlwind of a project given me by God.

I am thankful for loving parents who taught me right from wrong. And grateful for my mother's gentle nudging to record these stories years ago.

I thank my family and friends for their encouragement and technical support, and especially my grandchildren, who never ceased to insist on, "It's storytime, Memaw!"

Words are inadequate in expressing how thankful I am for my illustrators and their terrific artwork.

I am equally thankful for my family, church family, friends and prayer warriors who prayed God's will be done.

Get Out of the Way!
Memaw Is on a Mission for God!

I love for Memaw to tell us stories. She says these are God's stories because He answered her prayer for them. Memaw wants us to learn more about Jesus. She would say, "These are God's stories and He's using me to tell them."

I think my Memaw is special because she prays all the time for her family. My name is Westin, and my sister is Jaidyn. We are two of her ten grandchildren. We stayed with Memaw and Pawpaw all the time growing up. We constantly begged her to tell us stories. We would chant together, "It's storytime, Memaw!" until she told us a story.

Memaw began recording some of the stories when I was about five because Nanny, my great-grandma, told her she should. I'm glad she did. Memaw teaches us not to put God in a box.

God is a big, big God. She would ask, "Did you just put God in a box? Get Him out of there!" Even I know you can't put God in a box because He is everywhere.

But now I get it. This is about Memaw. This is her testimony.

My Memaw is old. Some days she can hardly walk. Some days are much worse, but she gets over it. She says, "I'm not putting my God in a box. He can still use me to do something for Himself." Boy, is God using her for something right now.

I'm ten now. Eleven days ago, Memaw decided to type up and print out the collection of stories she had told us from her journal. She planned on having us read them to her on vacation. I would rather she just told us new stories. That night, she printed out seven old stories, and after church, she ran home and started printing out more.

On Monday, Memaw prints more; she couldn't stop. She was praying all the while. During one of those prayers, she was overcome with the Holy Spirit. God told Memaw to combine the stories and publish His book. "This is God's book,

His stories," she would say. It doesn't get any better than that.

Talk about last minute, on Saturday morning God led Memaw to ask our pastor if she could speak before the congregation the following day, Sunday. She wanted our church family to know the miraculous thing God was doing. The pastor told her he would like to meet with her before Sunday school to discuss it. She prayed it would be this Sunday.

Memaw called her friends and family and told them, "God is performing a miracle." Memaw spoke to Pastor Sunday morning. She explained all that had happened and read him two of her stories. He was pleased and told her he would buy her first book. Memaw told Mommy, "This day will go down in infamy."

After the sermon and invitation were given, Pastor called Memaw to the pulpit and handed her the microphone. Mommy recorded it all on her cell phone. Memaw was so excited, she tried to run to the pulpit. That's the fastest I've seen her move in years. She was overwhelmed with excitement and gratitude that God was using her, a nobody with no creative mind, to open the hearts of kids. She wants every child to know how much God loves them, how He desires their whole heart.

Memaw spoke of the miraculous thing God was doing. I could tell she was nervous, but she settled in quickly. After bringing the church family up to date, she read, "Can Anyone Beat Joe?" It's the next story in this book. It's a true story about my great-grandfather, Joe, when he was in the sixth grade. Everyone in the church gasped at one point. We all laughed a couple of times. My great-grandmother, Nanny, got emotional. My great-grandfather, Joe, died a few years ago and is with Jesus right now. I'm named after him.

After she finished telling the story, people began clapping, but Memaw stopped them. She said, "Don't clap for me, but if you want to praise God, feel free, because this is God's doing." She raised her hand toward heaven and said, "Now you can clap, praise, praise the God that we serve." Wow!

Monday, Memaw had to get organized. She had papers all over the place. They were flying off the printer, falling on the floor, and stacked all over the kitchen table. God was steadily giving her new stories, too. She couldn't type them out quick enough. She thought each one was the best. Of course, because they were from God.

Memaw went and visited a publisher and talked about self-publishing. Then she spoke with a Samaritan's Purse volunteer, who had published books, and asked what steps she took to publish her books. All the information was too confusing.

Memaw prayed, "I don't know what to do, but You do. I'm trusting You. I believe you want these stories that glorify You in the hands of Your children quickly. I see the sign of the times. Your coming is at hand. How do I do it? Help me." With that, a godly family in business came to mind. She asked, "God, do You want me to call them? I'm going to call."

Memaw called and was thrilled someone answered. Many businesses were working shorter hours or closed completely due to a viral outbreak. After speaking to the lady, Memaw needed to leave immediately. The office would close in five hours and it would take at least four and a half hours to get there. She had no time to spare.

Memaw snatched up a handful of God's stories hot off the printer, grabbed her purse, pottied, kissed Pawpaw goodbye, and flew out the door. "I've got my phone! I'm on a mission for God!" She set the navigation system in the car and blasted off. She called some close friends. "Please pray. I must get these stories delivered by five o'clock. The children of the world need these papers now. God wants them to be ready for His coming." They prayed God's will be done.

Christian music was blaring on the radio. Memaw sang along with arms raised in praise, soaking in His goodness. She sang, "Smile," "Let it Rain," "Almost Home," and "I'm Going to See the Victory"—those songs and many others. Each spoke to her heart. It was awesome. Memaw had to succeed; she didn't want God to raise up someone else to do His work. She won't put God in a box. He can do exceedingly amazing things through her because she believes.

In her excitement, she was driving way too fast. She assumed it was okay to speed because this was for God. It must be done. She couldn't be late. Then she was convicted to slow down; it wasn't okay. Memaw took her foot off the gas pedal. It's too late!

A cop raced up behind her. Memaw was startled to see blue lights flashing and shocked to hear sirens. Memaw's getting a ticket. Pawpaw is going to be mad. He doesn't like her driving much anyway. Memaw pulled over and hit the brakes, throwing dirt and gravel everywhere.

She skidded to a stop.

The police officer comes to the window and in a deep voice slowly says, "Ma'am…"

She answers immediately, "I'm on a mission for God. These are His papers, and I must deliver them by five o'clock. The little children of the world need them now. Jesus is coming soon! They need to be ready!"

The officer looked skeptical. "You say those papers are from God? Show me."

Memaw held the papers out of her car window and pointed. "See? They say, 'From God!'"

The officer was shocked. He couldn't believe it. "Grab your purse, get God's papers, lock your car," he said. "Get in mine. Buckle up. Let's go. I'll get you there on time. This is a true emergency."

Memaw grabbed her purse and the papers from God. She bailed out of her car and locked the car door. Memaw jumped in the police car and buckled up. The police officer turned on the lights and sirens. She saw the lights reflecting off the other cars. The officer was zipping in and out of traffic with lightning speed. People got out of their way. Memaw was glad. They weren't breaking the law now.

They arrived at the office at 4:58 p.m. They made it with two minutes to spare. Memaw was relieved and thrilled as she delivered God's papers. Now the little children will get the very important information sent by God.

Be watching, Jesus is coming soon!*

Jesus said, "Let the little children come to me, and do not hinder them, for the kingdom of heaven belongs to such as these."

Matthew 19:14 NIV

1.

Can Anyone Beat Joe?

Joe went to school with his pal Bill. They talked every day. Bill was the most cheerful guy Joe had ever met. This really puzzled Joe.

The boys were in the sixth grade. Joe was a strong muscled-up kid. He was very competitive. He was taught to do his best in everything. Joe did his best mowing the grass. He did his best cleaning his room. He did his best in school. And Joe especially did his best in sports. He loved football, wrestling, baseball and boxing. The school had competition in all of these events, including swimming.

Joe would beat everybody. He won the boxing tournament and the wrestling tournament. Joe could outrun all the boys in track. As the running back, when Joe got the football and ran, no one could stop him!

With being so good in school and in sports, you would think Joe would be happy. He really wasn't. Something was missing. Joe wanted to be happy like Bill. There was something different about Bill.

When it came to swimming, Bill came in first. Joe always placed second. He couldn't understand it. Joe would move his arms as fast as he could and kick his legs with all his might. No matter how hard he tried, Bill still won. How could Bill beat Joe? Bill was born without legs! When he swam, Bill had no legs to kick with.

How could Bill be so happy? He couldn't play football or baseball. He couldn't box. Joe felt so sorry for Bill. But Bill was always smiling, especially when he would beat Joe swimming. It was cool having all the kids in school talk about Joe losing to Bill.

Bill would laugh a bit, and say, "Hey, Joe, guess you can't be the best in everything, huh?"

Joe couldn't stand it any longer. He abruptly and rather sternly asked, "Bill, how can you be so happy all the time? You have no legs. You can't even play most sports. You have to use a wheelchair. That's nothing to be happy about. You should feel sad. I feel sad for you."

There it is again. Bill and his big smile. He chuckles. "Joe, think you can handle this?"

"Of course, I can!" Joe insisted.

Bill explained, "You're right. I wasn't this happy all the time. Several years ago, before I met you, I was miserable. I was sad. I cried a lot. I kept asking God, Why me? Why didn't You give me legs? I really want to run and play and do all the things that you do, Joe."

"What changed then, Bill?" Joe asked.

Bill explained, "Jesus. Jesus happened. In all my moaning and groaning and feeling sorry for myself, I wasn't doing anyone any good. I hated myself and I was ugly to others. Finally, I just had a long talk with God. I realized that God does not make mistakes. And I realized that God is a jealous God. I have a purpose being born without legs. Maybe that's so I could beat you at swimming, Joe."

They both laughed.

Bill continued, "I thought about God being a jealous God. That meant I had to put Him first. I had a choice to make: put God above everything or put my circumstances above everything. I chose God. With that, I accepted Jesus Christ into my heart, and I am a **new** creation. A new creature. The 'old' me is no more. If you want the joy I have, Joe, you need to accept Jesus Christ as your Savior."

"I certainly do. I want to live with joy like you, Bill," Joe replied.

At that moment, Bill led Joe in accepting Jesus Christ as his Lord and Savior. They remained friends ever since.*

> *"These things I have spoken to you so that My joy may be in you, and that your joy may be made full."*
>
> John 15:11 NASB

2.

It's a Paper Fight—Throw! Throw!

My name is Melissa. Robyn was my best friend. We were in the sixth grade many years ago. We played volleyball and ran track together. I spent the night at her house sometimes, and she slept over at mine.

Robyn's parents were strict when it came to school. She knew she had to mind the teachers and make good grades. Robyn was a good girl and never got in trouble at school. That is, not until today.

This was a day like no other. Our math teacher, Mrs. Bee, was very lenient. She never got on to anyone. For days now, kids had been disruptive in her class, even me. It was fun. Joseph passed notes to kids three aisles over. Two boys in the back were standing up and telling jokes. Everyone was talking and no one was paying attention to Mrs. Bee.

Mrs. Bee began writing math problems on the blackboard. I noticed sev-eral kids tear out a piece of paper and start chewing it. At first, I couldn't figure out why. Shortly thereafter, I figured it out.

When Mrs. Bee turned again to face the blackboard, pieces of wadded up paper began flying through the air. They were hitting the blackboard. Some of them stuck; those were spit wads (paper wet with spit). They're disgusting.

We thought it was hilarious. Others joined in, and soon everyone was throwing crumpled-up paper. Wads of paper were flying everywhere. They were whizzing by on my left side, on my right side, and over my head. Some hit the ceiling and some were hitting the windows. A few would stick for a minute, then just fall off. That's when everyone roared in laughter. The floor was covered in pieces of paper. It was a wild scene.

I kept encouraging Robyn to throw one. Everyone told her to. We told her she was missing out on the fun. Robyn sat there and would nod no. The chaos went on for at least ten minutes.

In the excitement of it all, we were getting louder and louder. Robyn couldn't stand it any longer. She carefully tore off a piece of paper. She crunched it up. She put it in her mouth.

She chewed it for a bit. She took it out of her mouth. She took aim. Wham! She threw it, and it landed exactly where she wanted it to. She couldn't contain her excitement.

BAM! The classroom door flew open. "Robyn, Sandra. My office, **now**!" demanded our principal, Mr. Kline.

Robyn was in shock. All she could think of was, *Why? Why did I do that? I know better. My parents are going to be so mad. I'm in big, big trouble.*

Robyn and Sandra got up and followed Mr. Kline to the office. In the office, Sandra denied throwing a spit wad. Robyn couldn't believe it. Robyn knew Sandra threw at least a hundred spit wads because she watched her. The principal sent Sandra back to class. Robyn thought to herself, *What? Really? Unbelievable!* Robyn admitted she threw one, just one. She didn't lie. Mr. Kline gave her after school detention for three days. Robyn's parents were very upset and punished her too—no phone, no television, and no friends over for a week.

For days, Robyn was mad because she was the only kid that got caught. It wasn't fair. She truly was the most well-behaved kid in school. But really, Robyn was mad at herself for not being strong enough to do the right thing.

Robyn prayed, "Dear Jesus, please help me behave in school and have the courage to do what is right. I'm sorry for what I did. I knew better. You know I tried very hard not to throw a spit wad. I can't fight peer pressure on my own, but I can do all things through You, because You give me Your strength. Next time something like this happens, I'm going to imagine You sitting on Mrs. Bee's desk watching everything. I know You are always at my side. Amen."*

I can do all things through Him who strengthens me.

Philippians 4:13 NASB

3.

Pawpaw's Scared of Doctors and Shots

During spring break, Amy and I stayed with Memaw and Pawpaw. Pawpaw had to go to the dermatologist to have a rash checked out, and we went with them. Pawpaw hates needles. When he sees a shot with a needle, he gets all sweaty and turns pale. Pawpaw gets a real serious look on his face and can't smile. Poor Pawpaw. I think it's funny.

My Pawpaw wears a hearing aid and glasses. He has gray hair and a gray beard and loves watching old gray cowboy shows. While we waited to see the doctor, I begged Memaw to tell us a story. She thought a while and said, "Here you go Derrick and Amy."

* * * * *

Once upon a time, there was an old gray-haired man who wore glasses and a hearing aid because he couldn't see or hear well without them. His name is Vick, but the grandkids call him Pawpaw Vick. He likes to sit in his recliner with the TV clicker and watch old black-and-white cowboy television shows. He has a wife named Granny. They have ten grandchildren. (Amy and I laughed because we knew she was talking about them. She's so funny.)

One day, Pawpaw Vick came and sat on the side of the swimming pool. The pool was an above-ground pool, but Granny insisted they put it in the ground. So the whole pool is underground except for about two feet. It made a perfect bench for Pawpaw Vick to sit on.

Granny was swimming in the pool with nine-year-old Doo and seven-year-old Maye. She loves the water and swims like a fish. I think she was part fish. She loves soaking in a tub or being out on the water in a boat.

Doo and Maye started begging Pawpaw Vick, "Pawpaw, please come swimming with us? It's fun. Please, Pawpaw, please?"

Pawpaw Vick always said, "No, not today." He was afraid he would get cold.

Doo thought, *How can Pawpaw Vick get cold? It's 100 degrees out today.*

Summer heat in South Louisiana is miserable.

About that time, Pawpaw Vick's hearing aid battery died. He couldn't hear. He said, "Darn it, my battery went dead. I've got to change it."

Granny is pretty crafty. She said, "Oh dear, just sit there. I'll get it for you." She quickly jumped out of the pool and patted down with a towel. She said, "Honey, give me your hearing aid and glasses. I'll take care of this and bring out your sunglasses."

Pawpaw Vick gave Granny his hearing aid and glasses.

She zipped into the house.

Doo and Maye jumped out of the pool and stood by Pawpaw Vick. They were all talking.

Granny replaced Pawpaw Vick's hearing aid battery and found his sunglasses, but she sat them down on the table by the patio doors. Next thing you know, Granny comes out and jumps back into the pool. She swam up behind Pawpaw Vick. Pawpaw Vick didn't know what was going on. Granny could see Doo and Maye, and they could see her, but Pawpaw Vick couldn't. She was making hand motions for the kids to flip Pawpaw into the pool.

The kids understood and started laughing.

Pawpaw Vick asked, "Babe, where's my glasses?"

Doo and Maye each grabbed one of his legs. They started laughing so hard.

Pawpaw Vick started kicking and yelling, "Hey, hey, stop that!" He was trying to kick his legs free. BAM! Pawpaw Vick did a big back flip right into the pool and went completely underwater.

Doo was laughing so hard. Maye was laughing too, and she jumped back into the pool. Granny thought it was hilarious.

When Pawpaw came up for air, he wasn't laughing. He hollered, "Don't ever do that again! You hear?"

Doo continued to laugh and Pawpaw Vick tried to grab him, but missed. Doo falls on the ground and laughs hysterically, "Pawpaw Vick, you're too slow. Pawpaw, you know you can't catch me. I'm too fast."

Then Pawpaw Vick tried to catch Maye in the pool, but she said, "I don't think so, Pawpaw Vick. I can swim fast." She went underwater and got away.

Pawpaw Vick looked at Granny. She was smiling so big.

Maye swam up to her and said, "Look at Pawpaw Vick. He's finally in the pool. Come on, Pawpaw, play with us."

About that time, Doo ran and did a huge cannonball into the pool. Water splashed everywhere!

Pawpaw Vick thought about God's Word; children are a gift from Him. Pawpaw prayed silently, *Thank You, Lord, for our children and grandchildren. They are so innocent and fun to have around. Help me and Granny teach them about You. Give us Your wisdom in caring for them. Mostly, thank You for Your Son, our Savior, Christ Jesus. Amen.*

Eventually, everyone got out of the pool. Pawpaw Vick sat under the patio with Doo. Maye went to get popsicles out of the freezer in the garage. She's like a little momma and tries to take care of everybody. Maye got a red one for Pawpaw, a blue one for Doo, and a coconut one for Granny and herself.

Before Maye came back with popsicles, Doo asked, "Pawpaw Vick, will you take us riding on the golf cart while we eat out popsicles?"

Pawpaw Vick asked, "Who, me?" No one else was present.

Doo had to ask, "Pawpaw Vick, is that why Granny asks if you have a mouse in your pocket?"

Pawpaw Vick smiled and shook his head; he didn't answer.

* * * * *

I told Memaw, "That story was a good one, Memaw." Then I said, "Amy! We are going to have to figure out how to REALLY get Pawpaw into the pool!"

"Yeah, Derrick. Let's make a plan. Pawpaw, you better watch out!" she answered.

* * * * *

Just then, the doctor and nurse came into the exam room. Pawpaw looked pale. The doctor checked out the rash on Pawpaw's arm, but then noticed something by his ear. The nurse led us all to the surgery room. Pawpaw was scared.

When we all got into the surgery room, Pawpaw was instructed to sit in a special chair. The nurse began gathering needles, medicine and cleaning supplies.

I was grinning as I walked up to Pawpaw. "Pawpaw, it's been real nice knowing ya," I said as I patted his chest. "I'll see you on the other side, okay?" Then I chuckled.

Pawpaw just made a face like he couldn't believe I just said that.

Then little Amy went up to Pawpaw. She sweetly and gently patted Pawpaw's hand and softly said, "It's okay, Pawpaw. You're going to be all right. Jesus is with you, Pawpaw, because He said He would never leave us."

Pawpaw couldn't believe how sweet she was. He was glad she knew Jesus is always with us, no matter what. She knows He's with us when we are sad, scared, mad, hurt, glad and being ugly. He's with us all the time!

The doctor came into the surgery room and walked straight to Pawpaw. He started cleaning Pawpaw's skin. Memaw had me and Amy sit right beside her in the corner of the tiny room. No one was laughing or joking now. We watched the doctor take care of Pawpaw. He took a biopsy in less than two minutes. Pawpaw did well and was ready to get out of there. Afterward, we went out for pizza.*

A joyful heart is good medicine, but a broken spirit dries up the bones.

Proverbs 17:22 NASB

4.

Hamburgers and Fries to Go, Please

Summertime is here. It's too hot to play outside right now. The temperature is 101 degrees but feels like 116 degrees. My name is JoAnn. Mary, Cissy and I were cooling off inside Mary's house. We had ridden bikes earlier and pedaled out to the pier. What a rare sight to see.

The bay looked like glass, like a mirror really. It was absolutely smooth, no ripples and no wind either—just hot. The bay was on fire.

The fury of at least fifteen pelicans dive-bombing the water was spectacular. They circle high in the air. They take aim. Two or three would dive straight down. BAM, BAM, BAM! They make a huge splash when they hit, and the sound it makes was stunning. The pelicans scoop up their targeted meal and then rest as they bob a bit on the water.

BAM! Another one hits the water. BAM, BAM! Two more hit the water.

I like to look for God in everything because He is in everything. The beauty of God's creation cannot be matched.

We were bored. Mary grabbed the phone, and we started making prank calls. We called people and said the

most ridiculous things. "Just reminding you of your doctor appointment tomorrow with Dr. Ferring," announced Mary.

The poor lady would say, "Honey, I don't have an appointment with Dr. Ferring."

Mary told her, "Oh, yes ma'am, you do, Mrs. Edmonds," then hung up.

We roared.

Then it was Cissy's turn. She called the drug store and asked them what movies were playing today. She hung up before they could say a word. We couldn't stop laughing.

My turn now. I call the local café. I didn't know my aunt had started working there. I thought that sounded like her voice on the phone, but it couldn't be. I disguised my voice the best I could and said, "My name is Mrs. Sayers. I need five hamburgers with fries and five Coca-Colas to go, please. I'll be there in twenty minutes to pick it up. Here's my number..."

We found this to be extremely amusing.

We had cooled off, so we went out to ride bikes again. Dusk was falling rapidly, so we all split up and I headed home.

What a wonderful day, I thought.

I put my bike in the garage and walked inside. When I went into the living room, I heard Mom on the phone. She was saying, "I'm so sorry. We will make it right. I'll be there in about twenty minutes." Click. "JoAnn! You get in here right now!"

I came running. "Yes ma'am. What's wrong, Momma?" I asked.

"Did you call the local café and order burgers for Mrs. Sayers?" she asked.

What could I say? I have to tell the truth. Why is she so mad? It's not a big deal. "Yes," I answered.

We loaded into the car right away and took off.

"When I get you there, you will apologize. I will pay the bill, but you will work it off. I am so disappointed in you, JoAnn. Why would you do such a thing?"

I really couldn't tell her it was fun, it was hysterical; we had a ball. I answered, "I don't know. We thought it was fun."

Mom said, "Do you realize those people worked hard making five burgers and fries, and to have them ready at five p.m. during rush hour? When they called Mrs. Sayers, she had no idea what was going on. Now she knows it was you. Are you proud of yourself?"

No, I wasn't proud of myself. The fun I thought I had was nothing compared to this.

Mom pulled up to the café, and we went in. The bill was $30.42. Mom paid it.

I said, "Mrs. Carson, I'm sorry for pulling the phone prank. We thought it was fun at the time, but it's not funny at all now. I'm so sorry. It will never happen again."

Mom drove us back home. Dad's filthy work truck was in the driveway. He works construction. Mom went straight to him and informed him of all that I had done today.

Dad was more than upset—he was mad. He called for me.

I came running, "Yes sir?"

With a stern face, he ordered, "Get out there and wash that work truck inside and out. You are going to work hard for that thirty dollars and forty-two cents. I'm so disappointed in you."

At least it was cool outside now. While I washed the grimy, muddy truck, I couldn't stop sobbing. That was probably the dumbest thing I had ever done. Working all alone slapping a soapy sponge on the tailgate, I thought about Jesus. I began praying. I asked for forgiveness. I told Jesus I never wanted to wind up in a mess like that again. *Please help me make better decisions and do right. Amen.*

I thought about His Word. The Bible says, His "mercies are new every morning: great is thy faithfulness" (Lamentations 3:23 KJV). I was comforted knowing that tomorrow is a new day; His mercies will be new.*

The steadfast love of the LORD never ceases; his mercies never come to an end; they are new every morning; great is your faithfulness.

Lamentations 3:22–23 ESV

5.

Jesus Is Coming, Jesus Is Coming!

Wes and Jasmine sat with Mom, Dad and Memaw at church every Sunday. Sometimes, they didn't pay attention or didn't understand the sermon. Memaw would try to explain what the preacher spoke on when they visited. She prayed a lot for her family and for lost souls.

Memaw would say, "There are lost people out there and we need to pray for them."

Wes asked, "Why do you say 'lost people,' Memaw?"

She loved it when they asked questions.

Memaw explained, "Sheep are weak. They are frail. They can't fight off lions and bears. They need a shepherd. A shepherd leads and protects and provides for his sheep. He loves his sheep so much that he will even risk his life to save them. Jesus is our Great Shepherd.

"David was the youngest of the sons of Jessie. As a young boy, he was a shepherd. David spent all day with his sheep, every single day. He loved his sheep, and his sheep loved him. You see, they knew he was a good shepherd because he took care of them. Like Mom and Dad take care of you. If a bad man tried to get you, your mom or dad would do anything, anything to protect you! David talked to his sheep all the time. They knew his voice. David also talked to God about everything, and even sang songs for Him. David had tremendous faith in God and knew one day he would be king just as God had said.

"David once chased a bear trying to get his sheep and attacked it. They fought. Imagine, a kid fighting and killing a bear that tried to eat his little lamb. David wasn't about to let that happen. Later, even a lion came upon David and his sheep. It walked up sneaky like a cat ready to pounce on an unsuspecting bird. The lion wanted to devour them. Eat them!"

Wes said, "That's like the devil. That's what he wants to do us, but we have Jesus. David is like Jesus because Jesus won't let the devil get us."

Memaw answered, "It's sad, but a lot of kids and a lot of parents don't know our Shepherd's voice. If the devil were to come today to harm them, what would happen?"

Wes answered, "The devil would hurt them because they don't know or call upon Jesus like we do."

"Absolutely," Memaw answered, with a great sense of joy. "The lion pounced! The fight was on. David and the lion were furiously rolling about on the ground trying to kill each other. Dirt was flying everywhere. Then suddenly, they both went limp. David pushed the dead lion off and threw him as if he were a bug. He yelled, 'Not my sheep, you devil lion!

They know my name, and I know them. No one or nothing will harm them!'

"Lost people are people without Jesus, our Shepherd. Those who haven't asked Him to live in their heart. They are like fragile, weak sheep without a shepherd to protect and care for them. The devil can devour them, torment them, make them cry, and make them do terrible things because they can't resist the devil on their own. Our Shepherd, Jesus, fights the devil for us. We call upon Him. The battle is His. Jesus is all-powerful, and the devil is powerless against Him."

Memaw asked, "But what happens to the lost people when they die?"

Wes answered, "They go to hell. That's where the devil will have to stay, too."

She then asked, "Do you think everybody in hell will one day make up and be friends?"

Jasmine answered, "On no, he's going to be mean forever. There's fire and stuff down there too, Memaw."

"Now, do we want anyone to live like that forever?" asked Memaw.

"Just the kid that keeps picking on me and making me miserable at school," replied Wes.

"No, no one should have to live that way," Memaw said. "Not even our enemies. Jesus wants all of us, all His children, in heaven with Him one day. Every person either makes the choice to accept Jesus as Lord and Savior, like you did, or deny Him as Lord and Savior.

"I'm waiting and watching for Him to return. Like y'all do when you know I'm coming. You are waiting outside looking down the street. I can see you at a distance. Jasmine starts screaming, 'It's Memaw. She's here. Come on outside everybody.' Everyone then comes out. One day soon, Jesus will come down from heaven riding on a cloud like that one right there." She pointed to the sky. "All that believe in Him will fly up in the air to meet Him."

"Wow," the kids said. "We are going to watch for Jesus, too."

For weeks, Jasmine talked about Jesus to kids at school, kids on the bus, and kids she ran into at Walmart. She would say, "Better be ready, Jesus is coming." Wes told a few. Some smiled and said, "Yeah, can't wait." Some said, "So what?" They didn't believe Jesus was coming.

Then it happened. After hundreds and hundreds of years, it happened. After people were told the gospel, told Jesus would return, told to be ready, told to wait and watch, it happened! "Jesus is coming! Jesus is coming. Mom, Dad, He's coming!" the kids screamed with joy. Jesus was riding on a cloud, shining brightly in all His glory. They jumped with excitement and screamed, "He's here! He's here!"

Memaw said, "Hallelujah."

Jasmine yelled, "Mommy, look, we've all changed!" as everyone flew up with thousands of others to meet Jesus in the air.

Be waiting and watching, for He will come. And it will be soon!

"You also must be ready, because the Son of Man will come at an hour when you do not expect him."

Luke 12:40 NIV

For the Lord himself shall descend from heaven with a shout, with the voice of the archangel, and with trumpet of God, and the dead in Christ will rise first. Then we who are alive and remain will be caught up together with them in the clouds to meet the Lord in the air, and so we shall always be with the Lord.

1 Thessalonians 4:16–17 KJV

6.

Is God Talking to Jody?

Jody and her brother walked to church every Sunday morning for Bible study and stayed for church. Jody liked going to the tiny church just down from her house. She especially loved the singing. She didn't think she sang well, but she knew God loved it. She knew this because she learned a scripture that said to sing praises to God four times!

Jody knows all of God's Word is important, but when God repeats Himself, He means serious business. In that one verse, God repeated sing four times. He didn't say sing if you feel like it. He didn't say sing if you sing well. We are to sing no matter what. That's a command!

An older man in church loved to sing, too. His name was Mr. Glass. Adults called him Joe. He had a low, deep voice. It was beautiful.

Someone once said, "He sings so awful, but it's so good. You know what I mean?"

Jody answered, "Oh yes, yes, indeed."

The young girl said "awful" because he sang so loudly. He had some pipes. Everybody knew when Mr. Glass was in church. He jammed along. At times, he would start to sing the wrong verse, but hurriedly got back on track. Mr. Glass had no problem with the chorus; he had those down pat.

The pastor preached. Jody paid careful attention. When the pastor offered the invitation and the music began, Jody's heart began to beat hard. It was a weird feeling and bothered her. It persisted. Occasionally, someone would meet the pastor up front and accept Jesus Christ as Savior, but not today.

The music stopped. Jody's heart quit beating hard. Oh, thank goodness. She felt fine. Jody went home and played with the neighborhood kids.

The following Sunday, Jody and her brother walked to church again. The older people always told them good morning with the biggest smiles on their faces. They liked to make a fuss over each and every kid. The sermon was good. The pastor spoke about God talking to Moses through a burning bush. Jody wondered why God didn't just talk to Moses like he talked to Saul Tarsus, the man who was also called (see Acts 13:9) Paul, the apostle Paul.

Pastor Bill offered the invitation. The music started. Jody tried to sing "Come Just as You Are," but she couldn't. The words just wouldn't come out. Her heart started pounding again. She felt nervous. She got scared. The music stopped, and voilà, she felt fine. She and her brother went home and ate lunch.

The school week flew by. After getting through the church doors this Sunday and telling everyone good morning, Jody

and her brother found their pew and sat down.

Jody prayed quietly, "Jesus, please don't let the music make me sick again today."

Service opened in song. Jody and Mr. Glass belted out "I'll Fly Away."

Jody did fine. "Thank You, Lord," she whispered.

After the sermon, Pastor Bill offered the invitation. The music commenced. The congregation began to sing "Have Thine Own Way Lord." Oh no! Jody can't sing. Here it comes.

Her heart was pounding harder than ever. She was so nervous. Then it dawned on her. *God is talking to me. I must accept Jesus into my heart today. He's been calling for me to accept Jesus as Savior. I want to, but I can't walk to the preacher in front of all these people.* Then Jody remembered that anyone who denies Jesus before others, Jesus will deny them before His Father in heaven. "I can't deny Jesus," she whispered.

Help me, she prayed. Jody's chest felt as if it were about to explode.

Abruptly, Jody jumped up as if she were struck by lightning. It was spectacular. If she didn't have a grip on the pew in front of her, she would have just flipped right over it. As soon as she stood, she felt a sense of calm wash completely over her. Jody felt God's presence and was at total peace. She walked to Pastor Bill and asked for salvation—to be saved. They prayed, and Jody asked Jesus into her heart. The music stopped. Pastor Bill announced to the church that Jody had accepted Jesus Christ as Savior. The congregation began to clap and shout, "Amen!"

"Jody Maye Turner" is written on God's hands, and Jesus is preparing a mansion for her in His Father's house. We are His!*

Sing praises to God, sing praises; sing praises to our King, sing praises.

Psalm 47:6 NIV

But whosoever shall deny me before men, him will I also deny before my Father which is in heaven.

Matthew 10:33–35 KJV

...who also sealed us, and gave us the Spirit in our hearts as a pledge.

2 Corinthians 1:22 NASB

7.

Oh, the Glory of Our God, Hallelujah!

Once upon a time, Dottie moved to a tiny town in Texas. She joined the local church there. It was a big beautiful church. All those present were very nice to her. The preacher was awesome. He preached the Word of God and everyone read scriptures. Dottie loved singing praise songs each week. You could feel the presence of the Holy Spirit during worship. It was great.

Dottie invited her neighbors and people she met in town to come to her church. Some did, and she was well pleased. About five hundred people attended worship service regularly. You had to get their early to find a seat, if you wanted to sit by your family or friends. Many deacons had to gather to pass the offering plate, or it would have taken all day. People joyfully gave their tithe. Dottie could tell the people were happy by the smiles on their faces.

Then it happened. A hurricane came through, and the devastation was tremendous. Many in the congregation moved; they never wanted to go through that again. Some of the young adults had to transfer out of state in order to maintain their jobs. The congregation was dwindling. Now, only about 150 people were attending regularly and trying their best to maintain the huge church building they loved so much.

Those who remained continued going to services steadily, but it seemed they weren't as happy. Some didn't get along as well as they had before things started falling apart. In the midst of this, the preacher suddenly left the church. Immediately, a pastor search committee was formed to hire an interim pastor and search for a permanent pastor. The poor church didn't have enough volunteers or money to do all the activities now, as they did before. Sadly, even more people left the church and joined other churches that had more to offer.

Oh, but the faithful few who stayed! They prayed to God. God, the Creator of the whole universe. God, who held the moon and sun still in time, in answer to Joshua's prayer. To God, who knew before He created each of them, that they would be in this very shape, this very day.

Dottie made it a point to brag on what God had done for her or her family, each week during Sunday school. Many prayed for spiritual growth. Dottie especially prayed for spiritual growth. She prayed in the sanctuary, she prayed during Sunday school, she prayed at the Ladies' Prayer Circle, and she prayed at home. She would say, "You are a big God. You are an awesome God. Pour your Spirit out upon us. Help us to love one another and let Your light within us shine ever so brightly."

God moved in Dottie's heart. She was overcome by His presence during prayer. As she was doing what she thought was something for her grandchildren, God told her the same would be done for His children. Dottie was moved. God wants me to do this for His children, she pondered. She was elated. She presented her project to her church family. God was with her. Dottie would never have been able to speak before the congregation without Him.

At home, Dottie was overjoyed and basking in His love. But then, the devil showed up in a bad, bad way. People were getting sick all over the country. The sickness spread so easily, everyone was mandated to stay home. This went on for weeks and weeks. No one was allowed to go to church. Dottie missed her Sunday school class. Dottie missed worship service. She was determined the devil was not going to put Jesus' light out at her church. He was not. She didn't care how hopeless the situation appeared; God is God! Dottie believed God will shine His light ever so brightly at her church again. He will (future tense).

Dottie continued her work at home. She listened to Christian music on her radio. At times, she just had to get up and dance as she sang. She knew God was about to do a mighty work in her life and in the life of her church.

The doors of the church had now re-opened. The virus had passed. God's faithful children were thrilled to enter church again, especially Dottie. They all greeted one another and praised God for the great privilege to gather again. In Sunday school, following prayer request, Dottie wanted to jump up and tell everyone what God was doing in her life. She wanted to brag on her God, but she couldn't. She couldn't get a word in. Everyone present was excited and shouting out praise report after praise report. In the midst of tragic circumstances, they were all truly blessed. Everyone was overjoyed and glorified God. Wow, to think how a tragedy brought on such great joy. Dottie remembered His Word: He makes beauty from ashes (Isaiah 61:3).

After Sunday school, everyone headed into the sanctuary. Dottie was in the choir. She couldn't sing well, but that didn't stop her. The small choir of ten was now a choir of thirty-five. The congregation now more than doubled in size, too; everyone came with more of their family, friends and neighbors. As the choir director led the congregation in the first song, Dottie couldn't believe it. Those in the sanctuary were singing with excitement. With great delight.

Dottie prayed right then, "God, pour out Your Spirit upon us. May we glorify You."

Instantly, the sanctuary was filled with the Holy Spirit. The humble-hearted children of God were overcome with His presence. *A tiny piece of heaven on earth,* she thought. They sang praise song after praise song. Those three hundred or so people in the congregation sounded like a host of heavenly angels in song.

BAM! The church doors swung open. People flooded into the church. They came in droves. Where did they come from? Why are they here? What's going on? They began singing and laughing. All the deacons jumped up and began greeting

the strangers that were entering. The music continued.

A tall, thin deacon named Mr. Jimmy shook hands with the first family that entered. He said, "My name is Jimmy, and this is my wife, Lou. We are so happy you are here this morning." Then he handed them the church program.

The newcomer said, "I'm Keith. This is my wife, Kelly, and our kids, Beaux and Luke."

Keith explained, "When we saw that bright light shining down from heaven on this church, like when it shown down so long ago in Bethlehem on baby Jesus, we had to come. God is here. I will raise my family here."

When we let our light (the light of Jesus) shine ever so brightly, it draws others to Jesus. They see Jesus in us and join in praising and glorifying Him as well!

"For I will pour out water on the thirsty land
And streams on the dry ground;
I will pour out My Spirit on your offspring
And My blessing on your descendants."

Isaiah 44:3 NASB

8.

A Shark! A Shark!

Ann remembered her dad liked saltwater fishing best. He would say, "You always catch something." He taught her how to fish and catch bait. Ann was glad he taught her how to operate a boat safely. It took practice, but she got the hang of it.

Ann didn't have a worry in the world when fishing with her dad. They always had a good time fishing and telling stories of the old days. The beauty off coast was something else. The sun coming up over the water was spectacular. She looked forward to the smell of the marsh. They watched massive schools of fish pass right beside them as the tide changed. Dolphins and chattering seagulls were a given.

Ann and her husband, Michael, bought a bay boat. It was 19 ½ feet long with a Yamaha 115 horsepower four-stroke engine. It was quiet, and could get up and go. Powder blue and white in color, it was a sight to see. Ann thought her boat was the prettiest one on the water.

Michael liked freshwater fishing and didn't go with her off the coast very often. Ann wasn't much on freshwater fishing for "little fish." She took family and friends fishing off the coast sometimes, and many times went out alone. It was sobering to realize the danger involved when she took others out with her. She was glad her dad taught her well.

Not so long ago, Michael and Ann went fishing off Last Isle, Raccoon Point. Michael snagged a huge bull red. That's a male or female red drum fish over 27 inches in length. Boy, what a fight they had on their hands. It took both of them to reel it to the boat. One would hold the rod until too tired, and then the other took over. They were worn out from the fight to get it to the boat. It took over thirty minutes. The redfish was massive. She was so big, she wouldn't have fit behind the captain's chair, much less fit in their largest ice chest. They believed she had to be at least four feet long.

Ann took a picture of the monster in the water with their flip phone but forgot to hit the Save button, so I can't show you. They knew she wasn't good for eating, so they just cut the fishing line and let her go. They wanted her to have lots of babies. Exhausted from fishing all day, they headed home with an ice chest half full of fish to be filleted.

Fishing at Raccoon Point was exciting. Ann had to go back. The weather was predicted to be perfect in a few days.

She asked Michael to take her back. He told her he was sorry, but he was already obligated to leave town for a couple of days. Ann was determined to go anyway. Michael urged her not to, but she insisted.

At 3:30 a.m., Ann got up, packed, hooked the boat and trailer up to the truck, and off she went. When she arrived at the launch, it was still dark. Ann liked getting there early because she didn't like being rushed to put her boat in the water. It takes longer to launch a boat when you're working alone.

Ann took the rope attached to the boat and hooked it to the tailgate. She unlatched the boat tie downs and made sure the key was in the ignition. Ann backed the boat down the ramp and got out of her truck. The boat floated off the trailer. She grabbed the rope from the tailgate and went to tie it off on the pier. Ann heard a loud rushing water sound. It took her a minute to figure out what was going on.

Oh no, she didn't put the plug in the boat! The boat was sinking. Before she panicked, she jumped in the boat and cranked it up. She drove it up onto the trailer and kept the engine revved up until she winched it tightly to the trailer tongue. Then Ann hopped out of the boat and back into the truck. She pulled the boat out of the water, got out of the truck, and waited until all the water drained out. Once she put the plug into the bottom of the boat, she went back to the truck and did it all over again.

It was too dark to go out. Ann waited for the sun to come up. She baited up all her hooks and set each rod in their proper place. She got the net out and positioned it for quick access. Ann ate her snack and took her medicine. Not another fisherman launched as she waited for daylight.

The day was dawning. It was time. Ann cranked up her Yamaha and unhooked the rope from the pier. She put the rope away and put her visor on backward. Ann idled away from the marina. After clearing the no wake zone, she opened that motor up and trimmed it out.

Moving at a smooth 47 mph, Ann was admiring the beauty of the sun, the waterway and the trees that outlined the bank while it lasted. She set the coordinates on the GPS system every so often, just in case she needed to follow it on her way back in. It looked like a trail of dots on her Lowrance. Last Isle, Raccoon Point, was due south, just over 20 miles out toward the Gulf of Mexico.

Very little land was visible. The last hurricane has since washed it away. It's a good fishing site. Ann idled around to the Gulf of Mexico side, pitched her anchor, and cast out each rod. With three rods in holders and set, she picked up her favorite rod and cast it. As she hoped for a bite, she sipped a cold Coke.

It didn't get any better than that. Ann sat on the cushioned ice chest and talked to God a lot. She loved the beauty He created, and told Him so. Ann was thankful God gave her health and the courage to step out and do when others probably wouldn't. She knew Jesus was with her. She trusts His Word: "So do not fear, for I am with you; do not be dismayed, for I am your God. I will strengthen you and help you; I will uphold you with my righteous right hand" (Isaiah 41:10 NIV).

Ann wasn't timid, not one little bit. In a flash, all four fishing lines took off. The poles were whining. All the line was quickly pulled off each reel. Suddenly, she heard a SNAP, SNAP, SNAP and again SNAP! The fish are here. Yippee!

Just before she stood up to grab the poles to respool and rebait, fish were jumping out of the water; some were flying through the air. The splashing sound of the water was deafening. Suddenly, a massive dorsal fin came out of the water right at the bow of the boat. A huge tail fin followed. Ann thought, *That monster is bigger than my boat. Ann was petrified. That's a shark! A huge shark!* She couldn't move a muscle.

She prayed, "Dear Jesus, help me get out of here, and I will never come out here all alone again." It took her a minute or so to calm down and crank up that Yamaha. She quickly maneuvered around the submerged island and then opened that boat up. She was flying; only the prop was in the water. Her nerves were shot. After she got a few miles closer to shore, she relaxed and slowed down.

Jesus, she thought, *I'm not supposed to be afraid, but I was afraid.*

Ann realized Jesus was nudging her to safety. He gently keeps us on course. Just a few miles from the launch, Ann pitched the anchor and got down to the serious business of fishing for the second time. All of her lines were out again. Ann and God were having a good time. She began singing praise and worship songs at the top of her lungs. It was awesome.

Ann didn't catch her limit, but she did catch enough fish to have a fish fry. She thought, *God kept me safe, He allowed me to fish, and He made it possible for the family to have a fish fry. How awesome is that?* She broke out in prayer and thanked God for her many blessings.

The verse came to mind of Jesus telling His disciples to follow Him, and He would make them fishers of men. Ann thought, *Fishing is fun, but I should be putting just as much effort and courage in fishing for men, spreading the gospel; that's what He wants from all of us. I need to be telling others about Jesus. He's coming back very soon.**

> *"He* **laughs at fear** *and is not dismayed; and he does* **not** *turn back from the sword."*
>
> Job 39:22 NASB

9.

Safe at Nanaw's House

Long ago, in the 1960s and early 1970s, when I was very young, nothing was more fun than going to Nanaw's when a hurricane was expected to hit the Gulf Coast. We grew up by the bay, outside the tiny town of Anahuac, Texas. Yeah, Anahuac. It's pronounced "An-a-wak." Anahuac was named by General de Mier y Terán of Mexico in January 1831 after the ancient Aztec capital. That's all I know about that.

We were always given plenty of notice to prepare for a hurricane. Many times, we stayed home. I never knew then why, but now I do. Only a few hurricanes were predicted to be dangerous and come close, forcing us to evacuate. When the meteorologist reported Hurricane Celia's path, Dad made the decision, "Load up, we're out of here."

After throwing pillows and sleeping bags in Dad's pickup truck, my brother and I rode with Dad, and my two sisters rode with Mom. Dad let us steer the truck down the long straight road to Anahuac. My cousins loaded up in their light blue station wagon, similar to the one in *National Lampoon's Vacation* (a movie from 1983) and followed us on the long drive to Nanaw's house.

Nanaw was about seventy years old. Nanaw and Pawpaw Teten were my great-grandparents. They lived on a large dairy farm. Pawpaw Teten died when I was six. Many dairy cows, one mule, chickens, pigs, one dog and two outside cats lived on the farm. The house had a large kitchen and two bathrooms. Two huge bedrooms were on each side of the living room. The closets consisted of a nailed 2x4 in each corner of the room with embedded nails used as hooks. Both bedrooms used to house many twin-sized beds. Nanaw had a small bedroom.

Stairs led up into the loft. All the kids slept in the loft. We could stay up late and play without disturbing the adults.

Two huge cable spools, which looked like a big table, were in the backyard. A big mulberry tree hung over them. Mulberries ripen right smack in the middle of hurricane season. We loved them. All the kids would climb onto the cable spools and pick and eat tons of the berries. We all had purple fingers, purple lips, and purple feet.

The winds picked up. Eventually, it raged through violently shaking the mulberry, oak and sweetgum trees about. When the rain hit, everyone ran indoors. We stayed at Nanaw's until the threat of danger was over; usually two to three days. As soon as we knew our house didn't flood and had electricity, we packed up and went home.

On the way home, my brother and I rode home with Mom. She explained that Nanaw and Pawpaw's house was an old schoolhouse when they bought it. They reared their children and other's there. A huge school chalkboard remained in the kitchen. It was never moved. Every morning, Nanaw wrote a different Bible verse on it. Before anyone ate, they had to read the scripture. Older kids would pick up the smaller kids and help them read the scripture. After breakfast, everyone went to work. Each had chores to do—age appropriate, of course. Some fed chickens and some fed the dogs. Some milked cows and some picked corn. Others cleaned house, helped cook, plowed the field, planted the garden, or mowed grass. There is always work to be done on a farm.

Nanaw lived a long life. She was ninety-one when she passed. I was an adult. I didn't know many of the people that were at her funeral. I was astonished when Nanaw's eulogy was read. After Nanaw's last child was born at home, she was much too weak to get out of bed. Day in and day out for weeks, she was confined to her bed and unable to care for her family.

Nanaw feared God and prayed, "Lord, heal me and I will serve You all the days of my life." Then, she climbed out of bed, got dressed, and went to work. She praised God for blessing her, for healing her.

There was a great need for families to care for abandoned children. Nanaw called the foster agency. A four- and five-year-old, brother and sister, needed a foster family immediately. Nanaw and Pawpaw took them in. About six months later, they realized they could care for more children, so they took in two more. Every so often, they took in even more children. When children moved out for whatever reason, the agency would call and ask if they could take in another abandoned child. Nanaw and Pawpaw fostered many children and loved each of them.

My great-grandparents had taken in and cared for 67 foster children over the years, and 62 of them were present at her funeral. They refused to sit in the pews until all the family had taken a seat. Nanaw's foster children were overcome with gratitude for my Nanaw and Pawpaw's decision to love and care for them, when others wouldn't or couldn't.

God healed my Nanaw when she was young, and she was faithful to Him until He called her home. She loved many foster children and they loved her. Some stayed with Nanaw and Pawpaw less than six months, but others lived with them for years.

My great-grandparents knew their Bible well. They had faith in God and instilled in their children and foster children the importance of knowing His Word. God blessed her with long life and the love of many. I can't wait to see her again when I get to my heavenly home.*

Behold, children are a gift of the LORD. . .

Psalm 127:3 NASB

For even when we were with you, we used to give you this order: if anyone is not willing to work, then he is not to eat, either.

2 Thessalonians 3:10 NASB

10.

You Have to Do *What* before You Walk into Your Church?

Brandon invited Wyatt to go to church with him this Sunday. Wyatt was excited to go. On Sunday morning, Brandon and his dad, Mr. Otto, stopped and picked up Wyatt. After telling everyone good morning, Wyatt buckled up, and off they went.

Mr. Otto parked the car. Everyone bailed out and headed for the church doors. Wyatt followed Brandon since he had never attended this church before. In a flash, Brandon jumped up, flipped around, and counted out loud. "One, two, three." By then he was facing Wyatt. Brandon then turns and walks into his church. Wyatt thought that was the strangest thing he had ever seen.

Then Brandon's mom and dad did the same thing. They jumped up, flipped around, counted out loud, "One, two, three," then turned and walked into church. Confused, Wyatt followed suit and did it, too. Wyatt went inside and searched for Brandon.

After Mr. Otto found a place for everyone to sit, the family took their seat and got situated. Wyatt asked, "What was that all about?"

"What?" Brandon said.

"That jumping, flipping around, and counting to three before y'all came inside."

"Wyatt, you did it, too. Don't y'all do that at your church?"

"No, man," Wyatt said. "I did it because everyone else did it."

Church service started. It was such a good sermon. Everyone sang at the end. No one publicly accepted Christ as Savior today. Wyatt hoped everyone there was already saved and going to heaven one day. He knows Jesus is coming back soon.

Later that day, Brandon explained we jump, flip, and turn around to honor God. We count to three for the Father, the Son and the Holy Spirit.

Wyatt got sad. Why didn't his mommy teach him he needed to jump, flip, turn, and count to three when they went to church? This coming Sunday, Wyatt was going to do the right thing at his church. He wanted Jesus to be proud of him. He was going to have to talk to Mommy and find out why they didn't do as Brandon and his family do.

* * * * *

Wyatt and his family arrive at church. Wyatt's ready; he leads the way to the welcome center. Sissy follows. Mom and Dad are behind them. Memaw is a good way back, but she's watching what's going on. Out of the blue, Wyatt **jumps, flips** around twice, **jumps** up again, then **counts**, "One, two, three" out loud. It was hysterical. Wyatt looked like he was breakdancing. Memaw thought, *What in the world?*

Wyatt then explained that everyone had to do this to enter church. "It's for the Father, the Son and the Holy Spirit. Come on, do it. Do it now. Don't you want Jesus to be happy with you?"

Sissy yelled, "Yeah, but I'm not doing that!" Mom and Dad smiled. Memaw told Wyatt she hadn't jumped or flipped in years. She was glad no one else was around to see such a display. After church, they all went out and ate Mexican food. Everyone loves the cheese dip. Memaw went home after lunch.

She said her sofa was calling her name.

On the way home, Mommy told Wyatt never to do that again. She said, "Son, there are some things you just don't joke about. Going to church and flipping out is one of those things."

Wyatt answered, "I wasn't joking! I did that for Jesus, like Brandon and his family do. Why didn't y'all teach us this? Why didn't Memaw teach you this?"

When they got home, Mommy told Wyatt to get his Bible. When he returned with Bible in hand, she told him to start looking it up. She wanted him to show her where it says to jump, flip, turn, and count in order to enter God's house.

Wyatt began his search. He looked up *jump, flip, spin around*. Nothing.

He looked up *turn around, count to three*. Nothing.

He looked up *What must I do to enter God's house?* Nothing.

How could Brandon and his parents get it so wrong. He ran, yelling, "Mommy, it's not in here.

It's not in here, Mommy. Nothing about that is in the Bible."

Mommy explained that many times people do things out of habit. They have no idea why they do it. Sometimes people do things because they "think" it's in the Bible, but it's not. She said, "We obey God. We don't do things because some *person* says we should do them. We do what *God* tells us to do. Do you understand?"

He understood.

She continued, "Jesus poured out his blood for you. Jesus did that. His blood washed away our sins. The Bible states by grace we are saved through faith, believing the gospel, and it is not of ourselves, it is a gift of God. We cannot save ourselves; God saves us. A gift is a present to us. We don't work for a present. We can't earn it. When Jesus died on the cross, God himself ripped the veil into two pieces. When we pray, we are *in the throne room with God Almighty*. No one can separate us from Him. I picture that in my mind, kneeling at the feet of God. Like when you sit on the floor by Dad while he sits in his recliner. You talk to him, and he delights in you. That's how it is with God!

"Heaven is our eternal home today, right now. He calls us precious. Wyatt, you were supposed to hang on that cross. I was supposed to hang on that cross. Aren't you glad Jesus took our place and did that for us?"

Wyatt nodded yes.

"He did it so we wouldn't have to. That's how much he loves you—He died to save you. That's why we are here: to tell others about our loving Father back home, in heaven. Let Jesus shine, Wyatt. Through your heart, Jesus can light up the whole world if you let Him. Let Him shine!"

Wyatt won't be breakdancing at the church doors anymore. He's trying to figure out how to explain all of this to Brandon without hurting his feelings. God is pleased.

"Let your light shine before men in such a way that they may see your good works, and glorify your Father who is in heaven."

Matthew 5:16 NASB

I testify to everyone who hears the words of the prophecy of this book: if anyone adds to them, God will add to him the plagues which are written in this book; and if anyone takes away from the words of the book of this prophecy, God will take away his part from the tree of life and from the holy city, which are written in this book.

Revelation 22:18–19 NASB

11.

How Strong Is a Child of God?

"And I will bless those who bless you, and the one who curses you I will curse. And in you all the families of the earth shall be blessed."

Genesis 12:3 NASB

After returning from Israel a few months ago, a group of kids asked about the trip. I explained we had an amazing time. Upon our arrival, we were bombarded with information from our tour guide. It was overwhelming. He would say, "Four thousand years ago, this happened right here, three thousand years ago this happened on this same spot, two thousand five hundred years ago this happened, and two thousand years ago, this happened." It was deeply moving knowing we were walking in the steps where Jesus Christ had walked.

Jesus' short life in such a small country means absolutely nothing to many. It brings out hatred in others. Oh, but those that truly believe Jesus is the Son of God, to those who seek Him, to those who pray, and to those who genuinely desire a relationship with Him; to them **He blesses beyond our hopes and dreams.**

I asked, "If the shepherd boy, David, fought Spiderman, who wins?"

The children had to think. They knew God was with David when he killed a lion and a bear and a giant; but Spiderman has special powers.

After a minute or so, I answered and told them David does. He beats any superpower, hands down, regardless of their special powers.

I asked, "If all our superheroes were in a battle against David at the same time, who wins?"

They thought about it.

David still wins. Joshua beats them all too! Gideon beats them all as well!

An eighty-year-old child of God can beat them all, too.

One kid asked, "An old grandma can beat them?"

Yes, indeed. She has the power of God Almighty in her. Jesus lives in her heart. The power that raised Christ out of the grave to life lives in her and in you.

"Who fights our battles?" I asked.

They all answered, "God does."

"Who can beat God?"

A little boy answered, "No one, because He is God."

The smallest child there was a girl, and she replied, "Yeah, I can beat Spiderman, too, because Jesus fights for me!"

I asked, "Who is our real hero?"

"Jesus!" they yelled.

Jesus is not man-made; He made man!

"The LORD will fight for you; you need only to be still."

Exodus 14:14 NIV

12.

HELP! Rescued by the U.S. Coast Guard

Pawpaw Joe, Debbie, Phillip and I went fishing off the Louisiana coast. It was still dark when we arrived at the launch. Pawpaw Joe turned the truck around in order to back the boat into the water.

Millions of shad bait fish jumped out of the water as our headlights crossed over them. It looked like millions of dominoes flying and falling in a chain reaction. It was an astonishing site and sounded like shuffling cards. I watched those shad every time a truck pulled up to launch and shined its lights over the water's edge.

Dad launched the boat. We turned on the safety lights, lined out our fishing rods, found a place to sit and prepared for takeoff. Dad cranked up the motor and headed straight to a sweet fishing hole.

As the sun was coming up, its rays were partially blocked by dark gray clouds. It was a gloomy day. It began misting, then sprinkling. The light rain would stop after a few minutes, but then later restart.

I cast out the first line. I was always ready. Pawpaw was baiting his hook when suddenly something swallowed my hook and took off. Everyone looked with excitement as we listened to the "zinging" of fishing line being carried away. I knew better than to reel.

I let that beast tire itself out trying to get away. I knew I had a garfish or a big red. Redfish are fun to catch, and good to eat. Eventually, I reeled and reeled, and got it a few yards from the boat. It spun around and made a huge whirlpool in the water. It torpedoed off, but I saw it. It was definitely a bull red. I worked hard and eventually Phillip netted it and placed it in the 152-quart ice chest. One down.

Dad's line took off and then Debbie had something catch her by surprise and almost jerk her rod out of her hands. The battle was on.

The fish were coming so fast that Phillip decided to net them, unhook them, and rebait when needed. As soon as he got one fish off, he had to get someone else's off. Someone would holler, "Fish," or "We need bait," or "Get the net!" Phillip didn't know what to do first.

We caught redfish, speckled trout, croaker and flounder. Pawpaw Joe caught all the flounders. Flounder is the hardest fish to catch, and he was "the flounder expert." The fish were hungry, and I was glad.

The rain picked up. The wind picked up. The clouds were thickening. It lightly rained for a while but stopped again. The fishing at our honey hole had come to a halt—we had to make a move.

We zipped around to another small marsh island. The plan was to get out far enough to set the anchor so we could cast right on the shoreline. Just before we got to the spot to drop our anchor, the waves tripled in size, the prop hit mud, and the motor stopped. Seemed like two seconds after the motor gave out, the boat washed up on the tiny marsh island. The back of the boat was now stuck in tall marsh grass. The storm was upon us, and the rain began pouring. Lightning was popping all around us and the thunder was loud.

Good thing Debbie packed her cell phone. Pawpaw Joe called the U.S. Coast Guard. He reported, "I have four adults needing to be rescued," then gave them our coordinates. The coast guard announced they would be out to rescue us as soon as the present wave of severe weather passed; it was far too dangerous to come out at that moment.

Suddenly, my rod and reel started humming. That's electricity in the air. We could be struck by lightning. Lightning was popping even closer to us. The thunder was deafening. I got out of the boat because we were the tallest thing out there and the console had a metal bar that encircled it. When I bailed out, I sunk about three feet in soft mud. I quickly climbed back into the boat. The mud covering my legs smelled horrible. I stunk. The lightning became more intense and striking within yards of us. The rain was coming down in sheets. I was scared. I was at the bow of the boat and could no longer see Dad near the stern.

I silently prayed. "Please help us. You were on the boat with Your disciples when a violent storm came up. You calmed the wind and waves. You also rebuked the disciples for their lack of faith. Strengthen my faith. Though I can't see you with my eyes, I believe You are here. Though I don't feel your presence, I believe You are at my right hand. Though I don't know your plan for all of us right now, I believe

Your Word. You desire the best for us and tell us not to be afraid. Thank You, Lord, in Jesus' name. Amen."

I had to laugh. Imagine laughing out in a boat in the middle of nowhere in the midst of a violent storm. Only through Jesus is that possible. The devil thought he could get the best of me. He did, until I turned it over to Jesus. *Ha-ha,* I thought. *Now Jesus has him on the run.*

The weather got much **worse**. They called it the training effect. Waves of severe weather one after another. Out of the blue, the weather began to improve. It was raining very lightly and the lightning and thunder had stopped for the moment. The U.S. Coast Guard approached and instructed us to leave our belongings and board their boat.

We had to leave Dad's boat, and all those fish; so many fish. I really wanted those fish. It was very difficult trying get on their boat. The high waves were causing them to bounce about, and the current and wind were so swift that they had a hard time holding it steady for each of us to jump onboard. Once on, we were strapped into tall seats with foot bars and hand bars. We were preparing for a dangerous ride back to the launch where our truck was parked. The next wave of severe weather was beginning to hit.

We made it home safely. Pawpaw Joe went back the next day and hired a tug boat captain to take him out to get his boat. He sure hoped it was where we left it. Cho! Co! That's Cajun for "wow"! The boat was right where we left it, and all the fish in the cooler were still covered in ice.*

Thank You, Jesus, for protecting us and for taking away my fear during that terrible storm. Thank You for saving the boat and the fish. Mostly, Jesus, I thank You for Your mighty love for us all and for taking my place on the cross. In Your precious name I pray. Amen.

I have set the LORD continually before me; because He is at my right hand, I will not be shaken.

Psalm 16:8 NASB

And He got up and rebuked the wind and said to the sea, "Hush, be still." And the wind died down and became perfectly calm.

Mark 4:39 NASB

13.

Pray Now, Memaw! NOW!

Memaw was excited to take me and Brother on vacation to Kentucky this summer. Aunt Donna came with us because Pawpaw didn't want to go. We had to take two airplane flights to get there, and two airplane flights to get back home. Brother and I had never flown before. We watched the planes go overhead while we swam in the pool. We told Memaw over and over again, "We want to fly somewhere." Today was the day.

We got to the airport early and checked in. We boarded the plane and stored our luggage. Brother sat by Memaw, and I sat by Aunt Donna. It was exciting. The sound of the roaring engines got our attention during the flight check. Then we started taxiing out to the runway.

Memaw is scared of flying. The take-off is what she dreads most. She didn't want us to notice. She kept smiling and silently praying. I sat by the windows and watched everything; so did Brother. Suddenly the engines whined so loudly, but we weren't moving. Then, quickly, we took off. It was bumpy and jerky, and we bounced around. Finally, I could tell we lifted off land. I liked the clouds. I liked looking down on the earth. Lake Pontchartrain was beautiful.

We ate our snacks and drank juice. In no time, the airplane started going down to land. Right after the plane touched down, the pilot tried to stop it fast. It pushed me forward, I had to grab the seat in front of me. *One down, one to go,* I thought. We had a long walk to get to our connecting flight. Aunt Donna read a sign: "Average Walk Time Fifteen Minutes." We didn't have fifteen minutes! We started running like crazy people through the airport. Every time we came to a flat escalator, we jumped on it and kept walking fast. Memaw can't run. She can't walk fast either. Huffing and puffing, she assured us she would make it. She did, but just barely. We boarded the second plane. This time I sat by Memaw. It was a smooth flight.

We arrived in Lexington, Kentucky, the Horse Capital of the World. It was beautiful. Aunt Donna rented a big fancy SUV. We loaded up and headed to our Airbnb. We passed miles of horse pastures. Some of the horses wore a white mesh mask; we didn't know why. Our cottage was on a horse farm. It was surrounded by huge green pastures with clusters of large oak trees.

Horses were scattered over the acreage and separated by white wooden fences. We moved into the cottage—our home for the week. I stayed in a room with Memaw. Brother and Aunt Donna had their own bedroom.

Memaw took pictures of us on a big John Deere tractor parked near the horse barn. We walked around the property and looked at all the horses. They were pretty. The horse owners happened to come out to feed. We got to talk to them.

Brother asked, "Why do some horses wear masks, and others don't?"

The funny man answered, "We only put masks on the ugly horses."

Everyone laughed, except me. I thought that was a mean thing to say about pretty horses.

The woman explained that some owners use masks to protect the horse's face and eyes from insects.

Every day we went someplace new. The next morning, we drove north, passing miles of horse pastures, and visited The Ark. It was huge. I liked seeing how Noah lived and took care of the animals on the ark for nearly 54 weeks (377 days). That's just over a year. We stayed all day. It was great.

The next day, we went to several caves. The Crystal Onyx Cave tour was the best by far. We had never been in a cave before. It was damp and cold inside. The formations inside were bizarre. I liked it when they turned off the light; it was pitch-black and I couldn't see a thing.

On day four, we took the golf cart tour of Churchill Downs in Louisville. The famous Kentucky Derby horse race takes place here in May every year. We watched a film called *Secretariat* about the champion racehorse. Big Red was his nickname. We've watched the movie many times. Afterward, we went to the Louisville Slugger Museum and watched baseball bats being made. Brother and I were given a baseball bat at the end of the tour. They were little, and we swung them around like swords. Aunt Donna and Memaw didn't like that.

Sunday, we visited a local church. It was a big beautiful church with stained-glass windows. The inside was covered in decorative carved wood. But behind the pulpit was something I had never seen before. Pipes covered the whole back wall.

Memaw was excited. She told me those were organ pipes. The service started, but there were hardly any people there. I thought that was sad. Why don't people want to go to church anymore and sing to Jesus like me and Memaw do. Brother doesn't like to sing, either.

The music leader started singing a song we had never heard called, "Dem Bones." It was catchy tune. "Dem bones, dem bones, dem dry bones. Dem bones, dem bones, dem dry bones. The foot bone's connected to the ankle bone. The ankle bone's connected to the shin bone…" Brother liked it. He sang! He really got into it. We sang that song over and over again during the entire trip!

One evening, we went to an outdoor concert and listened to blue grass music. It's a lot different than Cajun music or country music or K-LOVE music. We all liked it. We did other things, but I can't remember them right now.

On our last day, we arrived at the airport and checked in. As we boarded the plane, Brother said, "I'm sitting with you first, Memaw." After placing our carry-on luggage overhead, we all got seated and buckled up. Memaw and Brother chatted. The plane started to taxi out.

Brother blurted out, "Memaw, we have to pray. Pray now!"

"Okay, are you nervous?" Memaw asked.

"Yeah, I didn't know what it was like the first time we flew, but now I do. Pray now, Memaw."

"Dear Jesus, make Your presence known to us. Help us not to fear. Help us to be still and know that You are God. With Your mighty hand, Father, just pick us up and take us home. For You are God Almighty, and nothing is impossible for You. In the precious name of Jesus, we pray with praise and thanksgiving for all that You've done for us and all that You are about to do. Amen."

Brother seemed satisfied. He watched a movie on his DVD player. One down, one to go.

*　*　*　*　*

Brother sat by the window next to Aunt Donna on our connecting flight. I sat with Memaw. When the plane began to move, Brother, from across the aisle, loudly said, "Memaw, pray! Pray now!" He was scared. When Memaw started to speak, Brother frantically said, "I'll do it myself! Put your hands together now, Aunt Donna! Dear Jesus, be with us. Give us good weather and smooth flight. Keep us safe. Amen." The people in front of us and behind us said amen, too. Brother was fine after that. Memaw was thrilled he called upon the mighty name of Jesus in his time of fear.*

"So do not fear, for I am with you;
do not be dismayed, for I am your God.
I will strengthen you and help you;
I will uphold you with my righteous right hand."

Isaiah 41:10 NIV

14.

A Story about Heaven

God doesn't tell us a lot about heaven in the Bible. Justin and Janet begged for a story about heaven. Janet said, "Heaven is a perfect place. Nobody will be mean to anybody and you can't get hurt there because Jesus is there and the devil can't come there."

"That's right, Janet," Memaw replied.

Then Justin said, "Just make up something, Memaw. Tell us a story. It's story-time."

Memaw said okay but wanted us to know it is purely make-believe. They understood.

* * * * *

Once upon a time, there was a little girl and a little boy who were with their grandmother. The kids called her "Grandma." Grandma loved that. Well, one day Grandma, Ken and Annalynn were walking to the store when something happened.

Instantly, they were looking at each other, feeling sensational. Grandma had long red hair and was so pretty. She looked like she was a mommy instead of a grandma. It was shining brightly there and so peaceful. The street they were standing on was shiny gold. Ken said, "Wow! This is heaven!" Annalynn said, "It is. It's heaven!" They were all excited and overjoyed.

There He was, Jesus. They were in awe. Annalynn ran to him, screaming, "Jesus, Jesus. I've missed you." She jumped up on him.

Jesus picked her up, laughing. "Annalynn, My child."

Annalynn grabbed his hands and said, "Jesus, this is where the nails were in Your hands. You did that for me."

Jesus smiled. "That's because I love you so much."

Ken followed and kept quiet. He couldn't believe he was standing next to Jesus. After setting Annalynn down, Jesus hugged Ken. Ken said that was the best hug he had ever had. He knew he was totally loved and accepted. *My Jesus*, Ken thought.

Grandma was on her knees; she couldn't speak at all. She was overwhelmed and had tears of joy running down her cheeks.

Jesus helped Grandma up. He said, "Marlene, well done." Marlene smiled.

Annalynn and Ken said, "Yeah, Marlene." It was too much fun. They saw and admired the angels. The songs they were singing sounded amazing. Annalynn joined in singing. The angels chuckled.

Jesus asked if everyone wanted to go see a bit of heaven and they all said yes. Jesus stepped back and held out his hands and motioned them outwardly, and said, "Go enjoy your new home. Your will never hurt again."

Wow! The beauty was unimaginable. Vivid colors everywhere. Flowers, birds, butterflies, and trees everywhere. Animals were walking around in lush green draped trees. The waterfall was breathtaking and sounded wonderful. Trees of all types stood up so majestically in different shades of green and blues. Oh, the sound of the birds singing almost made Marlene cry.

Suddenly, a bear ran up to Ken. When Marlene jumped, Ken said, "Really, Marlene? We're in heaven."

At that very moment, the bear spoke. "Would you guys like a tour of a piece of Jesus' kingdom?"

They answered, "Oh, yes."

The bear told them to get on. Ken and Annalynn were thrilled to climb on his back. Marlene thought all three would be too many. The bear tried to reassure her, but then decided to call his buddy.

A huge lion came right up to Marlene. "Hop on," the lion instructed, with a huge grin on his face. Marlene hopped on.

Of course, Annalynn had to change her mind. She decided she wanted to meet a black panther and ride by herself. Immediately, a black panther arrived, and she talked to him. Annalynn couldn't stop giggling. "Hello, Mr. Panther. How are you?"

He answered, "I'm fine."

Annalynn continued, "I'm Annalynn. Would you be my friend and take me on a trip with the lion and the bear?"

"Of course I will, my dear. Want to climb aboard?" he asked.

Annalynn climbed on and got set to go. Finally, the bear, the lion and the panther all said, "Are we ready now?"

Marlene answered, "Absolutely."

The animals took off running. Soon their feet left the ground. They were all flying in the air with eagles and hawks and tiny birds. Marlene didn't mind a bit.

She thought she didn't like heights, but this was beautiful. The six of them were talking.

The bear said, "Here, we have a volcano."

Ken asked, "Can we go down in the middle of it?"

"Sure," answered the bear.

Zoom. They flew down to the very bottom of the volcano. The humans got off the animals and walked around. There was molten lava flowing. The lava was beautiful, red, orange, and yellow in color. Ken reached down to pick up a handful. Marlene gasped.

Ken said, "Really? This is heaven. We can't get hurt." He shared it with Annalynn. She continued to giggle and showed her lava to the panther.

The lion asked, "How about a trip to the top of a mountain?"

"Oh yes," everyone answered.

He continued, "Would that be a sand mountain, a snowy mountain, a rock mountain, a blue mountain—"

Ken broke in. "A snowy mountain."

Off they went in lightning speed. The snowy mountain was beautiful. It was mostly white, but with a lot of blue-colored snow in it.

Speckled through all the snow were blue trees and different shades of green trees. They saw spectacular flowers of colors they had never seen before. Animals everywhere: white bears, black bears, brown bears, red bears, gray wolves, white wolves, brown wolves, black wolves, and birds of every color, and many more. And all the animals were smiling at them. The bears even stood up and waved. The birds began singing sweetly and the wolves began jumping around with excitement. The magnificence of it all cannot possibly be put into words.

Marlene asked, "How long will it take us to see all of heaven?"

All the animals laughed. They thought that was so sweet. Having humans arrive was so much fun. *Poor little dears, they have so much to learn.*

The lion answered, "You will enjoy heaven throughout all eternity. You will never see all of heaven. It is much to vast! You will never be bored. It is the greatest place to live of all time, and that's because Jesus is here. We get to live with Him forever." When the lion spoke the name of Jesus, all the animals knelt down in gratitude. Even they worship His holy name.

Surely goodness and mercy shall follow me all the days of my life; and I will dwell in the house of the LORD forever.

Psalm 23:6 NKJV

15.

Tom and Don:
The Lamb's Book of Life

Memaw came down for a visit and stayed at our house over a long weekend. Maye and I love it when she comes. Memaw tells us stories and helps us bake goodies. I'm excited. I'm watching for her SUV to come down the street. I see Memaw's car. "Maye, Maye, come on. She's coming down the road. Hurry!"

Maye came running, the whole time screaming to Mom and Dad, "Memaw's almost here. Bubba sees her. Hurry up, come outside."

Sure enough, Memaw drove up. She always had to smile when she saw us jumping up and down, yelling, "Memaw!" She got out of the car and squeezed us so hard. Everybody got a hug and some kisses.

I said, "I'll get your bags, Memaw, because I'm strong and you're tired." Her name is JoAnn. She's my mom's mother. Sometimes I cut up with her and say, "Ms. JoAnn, let me help you now, ma'am." Everyone laughs.

* * * * *

The next morning, Memaw took us to the zoo for a while. Later, we went home and baked cupcakes. Every evening, we sit on the swing. Memaw likes Coco, our dog. She brushes her hair with the dog brush. I had to say it. Yes, I did. "Memaw, it's storytime!"

Maye said, "Yeah, storytime, please."

Memaw sat there a minute, then said, "Let me think a bit. I haven't told a story in a while." Memaw bowed her head and prayed for a story that would glorify God.

* * * * *

This is the story of two very different identical twin boys, Tom and Don Thompson. Tom is super smart, but lazy and barely passes the sixth grade. Don wasn't as smart, or was he? He asked God for wisdom and studied hard. Don succeeded in passing the sixth grade, too.

The family went to church frequently. Both boys heard the same sermons. Don listened and took God's Word to heart. At the end of the sermon today, the pastor invited anyone wanting to be saved from their sins and accept Jesus as Savior to come forward. Something stirred in Don's heart. He had to respond. Don stood up and met with the pastor. He gave his heart to Jesus and accepted Him as his Lord and Savior. Don Thompson's name is written in the Lamb's Book of Life. Don's parents were so happy. They all went out for lunch to celebrate.

Accepting Jesus as Savior is the most important decision anyone will ever make in their entire life. Jesus loves us so much that He died for us. Jesus desires a relationship with each of us and wants us to live with Him forever. Tom attended church, sang songs, watched the preacher, and bowed his head if someone prayed, but Tom was just going through the motions. He never took God's Word to heart.

Tom and Don's parents promised each of the boys a car for their sixteenth birthday, as long as they did well in school. Don did well. He was thrilled to get his car. It was an old jalopy, but it ran well. Tom's report card was terrible; he got clothes for his birthday present. Don drove his brother to school every day.

A year later, Tom failed the eleventh grade and he didn't care. He was too lazy to do his homework. His mom and

dad were very upset. Don passed the eleventh grade and got a part-time job at the seafood shop during the summer. Don actually wanted to work and earn money. He was responsible for keeping fresh shrimp iced down and boiling crawfish daily for plate lunches. Don buys his own gas and earned enough money to fix up his old jalopy. Don now drives a really cool car.

Summer ended and school resumed. Tom repeated the eleventh grade. Kids made fun of him. Some asked, "Aren't you supposed to be the smart one? Doesn't your brother drive that cool souped-up car?" Tom ignored them. This time, Tom passed the eleventh grade while his brother passed the twelfth grade.

Mr. and Mrs. Thompson threw a huge graduation party for Don. All of Don's family and friends were there. Everyone congratulated him and told him they were proud of him. Don felt sorry for his brother.

* * * * *

"Wait a minute, Memaw," said Bubba. "They're twins. They are supposed to be just alike. How come they are so different? Don is doing good, but poor Tom's not."

"Yeah, Memaw, how come?" asked Maye.

"You see, guys, God made us all different. He gave us free will. Anyone can be taught right from wrong, but not everyone will choose to do right. I hope you see the difference and learn from it. Even if you are not smart, but have faith in God and pray to Him, He will help you through anything. And, if you are smart, but choose to be lazy, you will probably have a miserable life. It's your choice. Your mom can't make your decisions and neither can your dad. You have to make your own choices. So, would you say the smart thing to do is obey your parents and do your best in school?"

"Yes ma'am," they both answered.

"Well, I need to cut this short. I told Mom we would fry shrimp tonight."

"Oh, Maye dear, livid is the worst of the worst furious ever. It doesn't get any worse than that."

"Oh, he's in big, big trouble!" Maye exclaimed.

"Yes, dear, he is. Problem is, Tom doesn't think so."

* * * * *

Then his dad said, "My house, my rules. You don't think you have to attend school? You think you have the right to deceive us? You think you can just lay around and let your mother and I take care of you forever?"

Tom sat up and answered, "Yes, I do. I'm eighteen. I can do what I want, and I don't want to go to school or work or do chores. I want to watch movies!" Then Mr. Thompson said, "You follow my rules in this house, or you need to leave."

Tom not so smartly answered, "I make my own rules. I'm leaving. I'll live on my own." Mr. Thompson couldn't believe it. Tom has no money, no job, no food, and no place to live. Poor, poor Tom. Tom marched out of the house with the clothes on his back. His dad asked if he wanted to take extra clothes or food or—

Tom butted in and yelled, "No!" then stormed out the front door.

As Tom strolled down the sidewalk, he took notice of birds chirping and squirrels zipping around. A cool light breeze was blowing. It was a gorgeous day.

That night was a different story. The wind picked up, the temperature dropped, and it began to mist. Tom was cold. All the businesses were closed. He had no place to go. Tom just kept walking and happened upon the edge of town near the woods. For lack of a better spot, Tom walked a short distance into the woods, found a sparse area, sat down, and leaned up against a smooth tree stump. He was exhausted from walking all day and fell asleep almost instantly.

The next morning, Tom's growling stomach awakened him. He was hungry. The nearby McDonald's food smelled so good. Tom headed over there and eventually got up the courage to walk inside. Tom approached the crew member and explained he had no money but was very hungry. The supervisor had mercy on him and gave him two sausage biscuits and a cup of coffee. Tom was grateful and thanked him.

* * * * *

"Mercy, Memaw?" asked Maye.

"Oh yes, mercy. Mercy is not getting what we deserve. Remember the alphabet, *m* then *n* for mercy. Mercy is not getting what we do deserve, and that's good. Did Tom deserve free biscuits and coffee? No, he didn't, but out of their kindness, they fed him."

Bubba said, "Yeah, like Jesus. We don't deserve His kindness 'cause we are sinners, but 'cause He loves us so much He gives us grace, like living in heaven with Him."

Memaw answered, "I can tell you are listening at church."

"Yeah, Memaw, but to Mom and Dad and you, too," he answered.

"Remember the two *g*'s for grace and getting. Grace is getting what we don't deserve, and that's good, too. God is all about grace!"

* * * * *

That evening, Tom went to a hamburger shack and begged for a meal. The workers were kind and gave him a cheeseburger with fries and ice water. Tom was thankful and told them so. He ate as he walked back to the woods. The sun was going down quickly and the mosquitoes swarmed. They were terrible. Tom was constantly being bitten. He didn't sleep well. At times, he thought he heard an animal growl a distance away. That spooked Tom.

The sun had risen. As Tom walked out to the road, he saw a man coming out of the woods just down from him, wearing a bright orange vest and camouflage pants.

The hunter was carrying a big shotgun and yelled, "Are you hunting too?"

Tom replied, "No, man, I was just watching the animals and listening to the birds."

The hunter replied, "Did you hear that bear? I couldn't get out of there quick enough!"

Bear? Tom thought. That frightened him. He answered, "No, not really."

At two o'clock in the afternoon, Tom hadn't eaten a bite all day. He was starving. Aw, yes, pizza. *I want pizza,* he thought. Tom walked to the pizza place and expected free pizza because everyone else was so nice. He went in and pleaded for two slices of pizza and a Coke. Tom was stunned at what they said.

* * * * *

"What did they say, Memaw? Did they give him food? He needs food," said Maye.

"They said, 'No money, no service! You want charity? Go find a church. Get out!' People in the restaurant heard everything. Tom was so embarrassed, he ducked his head down and ran outside. He learned not everyone is merciful."

* * * * *

Two hours later, at four o'clock in the afternoon, Tom still hadn't eaten and was extremely hungry. He wanted to cry. Church was the answer; they have a food pantry. Tom walked across town to his church.

When Tom walked into his church, Ms. Jamie asked, "Hey, Tom, how ya doin'? Haven't seen you around lately. What can I do for you?"

Tom answered, "I really need some food, please."

Ms. Jamie had no idea what was going on, but she quickly and politely said, "Sure, come on to the food pantry with me. Here you go, let's load you up.

Vienna sausages? Tuna? Canned peaches?"

Tom nodded yes to each question. As Ms. Jamie handed him two bags packed with canned goods, he told her he wasn't living at home anymore.

Ms. Jamie said she was sorry to hear that, then asked if it was okay to pray with him.

Tom nodded yes.

"Dear Jesus, thank You for Tom. We love Tom and we know You do, too. Please take care of him and help us do whatever we can to help him. Amen."

"Thank you, Ms. Jamie," Tom replied.

"For I was hungry, and you gave Me something to eat; I was thirsty, and you gave Me something to drink; I was a stranger, and you invited Me in."

Matthew 25:35 NASB

Children, obey your parents in everything, for this pleases the Lord.

Colossians 3:20 NIV

17.

Tom and Don: Tom's Petrified!

Ms. Jamie from church was so nice not to make Tom feel bad and to give him food to eat. She gave homeless Tom Vienna sausages, tuna fish and canned peaches. She even prayed for him, and he said thank you.

I carried out the trash, fed my dog, gathered my dirty clothes, and took them to the laundry room. Maye is almost done with her chores. I hear Memaw. I'll be. She's sitting on the swing and yelling, "You guys better hurry up, or I'm just going to tell Coco the story."

* * * * *

Memaw began. Tom went to the woods again for the night but slept in a different area and stayed close to the road. The thought of a bear out there frightened him. He opened his bags of food that Ms. Jamie gave him and started eating. He ate it all. His stomach hadn't been so full since he left home. It felt good. But now, Tom was already thinking about what he would eat tomorrow.

Tom eventually fell asleep.

Suddenly, Tom heard a loud roar close by. *Oh my,* he thought, *it's the bear!* He wanted to run but knew that might be dangerous. He decided to play possum and not move a muscle. Tom really didn't know what to do. The roaring got louder and louder. Tom was trembling in fear. He saw two cubs scamper right by him.

He knows a momma bear can be vicious if she thinks her babies are in danger.

Then he saw it. A huge bear was right in front of him. The bear stood up on its hind legs with arms raised. It stared straight into Tom's eyes. The bear roared! It sounded like a freight train and hurt Tom's ears. Tom was petrified; he couldn't move. Tom zeroed in on the mouthful of teeth that could rip him to shreds. One swipe of the bear's paw could be deadly.

Immediately, Tom prayed silently. *Dear Jesus, help me. There's a bear! Please save me.*

Out of the blue, the bear fell down on all four feet, turned away, and walked on by.

What a relief! "Thank You, Jesus," Tom prayed.

Before, when someone led in prayer, Tom would bow his head, hum along, or just daydream until he heard someone say amen. Sometimes, Tom would even throw in an amen. He just followed what he saw others do in church. Tom believed in his head, but not in his heart. This was the first time Tom actually **meant** his prayer.

Some Bibles say a **fervent** prayer.

* * * * *

"What does *fervent* mean Memaw?" asked Bubba.

"It means that when we are right with God and pray a spirited prayer, a passionate prayer, God hears us and answers us. Tom prayed fervently, passionately, and God answered. Now, does that mean that God will answer our prayer right away, or in the way we think He should? Does that mean bad things will not happen to us if we do?"

Bubba snapped, "No, Memaw, they will. We know bad things can still happen. God's not a magician that makes all our wishes come true. God teaches us to depend on Him. Bad things happen to us so we will call upon Him to help us and trust in Him to get us through it. Like Job did. Now back to the story, please."

* * * * *

Tom got out of the woods and walked to the park, constantly talking to God. He said, "God, I don't like mosquito bites. I'm scared of big hungry bears. I want to go home. Please help me get home."

The sun was coming up. Tom was determined not to sleep in the woods ever again. That evening, he walked toward his parents' house. A great distance away, Tom saw his mom drive up in their driveway. Shortly thereafter, his dad drove up in the driveway. Tom wished he was home and wondered if his mom and dad missed him. Tom was starving. He'd had nothing to eat all day.

Tom gave his parents time to change clothes, chill out, cook, eat, and clean up. He wondered what his mom had cooked. No matter what it was, he bet it was good. After dark, Tom timidly walked up to the front door. He froze. He tried to knock. He couldn't knock. Maybe he just wouldn't knock. He was mad. His dad threw him out of the house. Tom turned around and walked away. Then he admitted to himself that his dad didn't throw him out; he had just left.

* * * * *

Maye said, "Memaw. I think Tom's mom would give him food if he asked for it. Don't you?"

"I surely do, Maye. But that's the whole point. He had to ask. Did they know he was outside? No. That reminds me, does God automatically save us and take us to heaven with Him when we die?"

"No. We have to ask Jesus to come into our hearts. He wants everyone to, but some won't. The story, Memaw," Bubba insisted.

* * * * *

Tom walked back to the park and sat in a swing all night. He looked up at the stars and thought about how many there were in the universe. Tom had learned that God knows each star by name. God truly is an awesome God. He told God he was sorry he hadn't accepted Jesus into his heart and that he was ashamed of how he treated his parents. "So, Jesus, I deny You no more. Forgive me of my many sins and please come and live in my heart. Thank You for dying for me and saving me. I want to live for You. Please help me be who You want me to be. Help me get home. Thank You for all the blessings You have given me, and thank You for what You are **about** to do. Amen."

As the sun came up, Tom got excited. He was going home today. He was going to eat a home-cooked meal. Tom believed God was going to get him home.

* * * * *

"That's *faith*, Memaw. Tom believes God will get him back home," Maye said excitedly.

Bubba butted in, "Yeah, yeah, we know that, Maye. Story, Memaw."

* * * * *

Tom waited all day. He watched his parents drive into their driveway from afar. He gave them time to cook, eat, change and all. Then he marched right up to the front door. He went to knock.

He couldn't.

Yes, he could.

No, he really couldn't.

He prayed, *Help me.*

This time when Tom went to knock, he was banging on the door. Mr. Thompson jumped. He was asleep in his chair in the living room. His mom thought, *Oh my goodness, what's wrong?* They both ran to the door and opened it. There was Tom.

Mom hugged him so tight. "Oh, Tom, Tom. Oh, come in. Are you hungry? I have leftovers. How are you?"

Dad couldn't get a word in. He eventually got to hug Tom. He told Tom he was so glad he was home. Tom felt welcomed and loved.

Tom ate three whole platefuls of food and was full. Afterward, Tom said he should leave. His parents said, "Oh no, Son, please stay. Your room is just the way you left it. We love you and have missed you so much. Won't you stay?"

Tom teared up and admitted he wanted to live at home again. He apologized for being an awful kid and happily announced, "I'm going to heaven with the rest of the family, guys. I'm a 'new' man." His mom and dad were relieved and so thankful.

Mom was glad Tom went upstairs to take a shower; he smelled awful.

* * * * *

Bubba couldn't help himself. "Memaw, that's like the Prodigal Son in the Bible."

"That's right, and just think how excited Jesus is now that Tom was lost, but now he's found." Memaw read from her Bible:

"So he got up and came to his father. But while he was still a long way off, his father saw him and felt compassion for him, and ran and embraced him and kissed him. And the son said to him, 'Father, I have sinned against heaven and in your sight; I am no longer worthy to be called your son.' But the father said to his slaves, 'Quickly bring out the best robe and put it on him, and put a ring on his hand and sandals on his feet; and bring the fattened calf, kill it, and let us eat and celebrate; for this son of mine was dead and has come to life again; he was lost and has been found.' And they began to celebrate."

Luke 15:20–24 NASB

18.

Tom and Don: Truly a Genius!

Tom was especially thankful to be back home. He slept peacefully for the first time in days. Tom's parents had already left for work that morning, and Don, of course, was at Louisiana State University. Tom got up, cooked breakfast, and ate. He thought about how he would complete his education so he could one day get a job. Then it hit him. Tom wasn't going back to high school; he was going to go straight to college.

Tom walked to the community college and requested to take the GED test, the high school equivalency test. The counselor encouraged Tom to sign up for GED prep classes, but Tom said no. He explained he could pass the test without studying for it. Tom took the test and aced it; no wrong answers.

The following day, Tom attempted to enroll in college and take courses to become a teacher. Tom would have to pass the SAT test first. Tom told them, "Great, let's have it," and took the test. He got every answer right. The college dean couldn't believe it. No one in history had ever scored 100 percent correctly. Tom truly was a genius.

Mr. Walker, the dean, came out of the office to meet Tom. He explained that because Tom was exceptionally clever, any college would give him a full scholarship to attend. Since Tom had no money, that was music to his ears. Tom requested to go to LSU and be in the same dormitory as his brother, Don Thompson. Mr. Walker checked into it. Tom was accepted at LSU and moved into dormitory room #15.

Don, his brother, lived across the hall in room #14.

Between classes, Don returned to his dorm. The boys ran into each other in the hallway and excitedly greeted one another. Both were overjoyed. They quickly caught up on everything that had happened over the last several months. Tom noticed a pretty woman walk into Don's dorm room and asked, "Who's that? Your girlfriend?"

Don explained, "Oh no, that's Ms. Sally. She's my English tutor. I pay her a hundred twenty-five dollars a session to help me with homework. I'm going broke, but I must pass the course."

"Fire her," Tom demanded. "I'll teach you. You can pay me sixty-five dollars a session. That's a win-win."

Don agreed and let Ms. Sally go. He was extremely nice about it. Ms. Sally understood and moved on to her next appointment. Tom helped Don every day. They were the best of friends.

Tom and Don graduated together three years later. Don received his bachelor's degree and is a physical therapist. Tom earned a doctorate degree in education and now teaches at LSU!

* * * * *

Bubba gave Memaw a thumbs up. "I'm glad Tom got it together. He really was a genius."

"For I know the plans I have for you," declares the LORD, "plans to prosper you and not to harm you, plans to give you hope and a future.

Jeremiah 29:11 NIV

94

19.

Life of Jimmy

Jane and Bob Jones had a son named Jimmy. Sadly, they didn't know Jesus. Jane, passed away when Jimmy was young. Jimmy's dad, Bob, lost interest in everything because he was so sad.

Jimmy wanted his dad to be happy. He behaved himself and tried to do everything he was supposed to do. Nothing seemed to please Mr. Bob.

Jimmy loved going to school and seeing his friends. He's away from home when he's at school. One day, Jimmy's dad got very mad and lost his temper. Jimmy left home. He really didn't know what to do; he just knew he couldn't stay home.

Jimmy missed his mom. He thought about her every day. Where is she now? Was she okay? Jane loved Jimmy. She loved to rock him when he was small. She enjoyed cooking his favorite meals. Jane would even pitch the baseball to him so he could practice batting. Jimmy felt all alone without her.

Jimmy slept under the bridge by the highway that first night. It wasn't comfortable, and he was a little bit scared. He thought, *How am I going to eat? Where am I going to take a bath? Are my teeth going to rot and fall out?*

Night passed and the morning arrived. It was a beautiful morning. Jimmy was hungry and had no money to buy food. Around lunchtime, his belly was growling. Later that night, Jimmy was starving. As he lay there under the bridge, Jimmy wondered how he could earn money to buy food. Then it came to him: He might could get a job at the nearby burger shop. They have good food and even serve breakfast.

The next morning, Jimmy went to a gas station and cleaned up. He hoped he didn't smell bad. He needed to make a good impression at the burger shop. Jimmy needed a job. He walked in, interviewed, and got hired! Jimmy volunteered to work every day. He made money and was able to buy his own food.

* * * * *

Every day, an elderly lady came in for a cup of coffee and sat inside and drank it slowly. She liked placing her order with Jimmy. She would always say, "Good morning, Jimmy." After a week or so, she said, "Good morning, Jimmy. Jesus loves you." She would say that several days in a row.

At first, Jimmy just thought it was nice. Finally, he couldn't stand it anymore. He asked, "Who is this Jesus? I've never met the guy."

Mrs. Clark kindly said, "Come sit with me on your break and I'll tell you all about Him."

Jimmy nodded he would.

Jimmy prepared to go on break. He grabbed a burger, fries and a Coke and sat down with Mrs. Clark. "Who is this Jesus?" he asked.

Mrs. Clark smiled. "Don't you know? He created you. He knows all there is to know about you. He loves you more than you can possibly imagine."

"No. I'm afraid not," Jimmy said. "My dad's name is Bob, and he's the meanest son of a gun ever. My mom's name was Jane. She really loved me, but she died when I was young. I really miss her."

"I'm so sorry, Jimmy. I can't imagine your pain, but I promise Jesus loves you. He created everything. He has a special plan for everyone, even you. You are no mistake. His Word says, 'YOU are fearfully and wonderfully made.'"

Jimmy didn't understand. He told Mrs. Clark, "I've got to get back to work. Can you talk to me tomorrow?"

"Sure, Jimmy. I'll be here," answered Mrs. Clark.

Jimmy went back to the bridge that night. He was thankful to have a full stomach. The night was clear and cool. It was great. He began thinking, *Who is this Jesus Mrs. Clark was talking about? I would certainly like to meet Him.*

* * * * *

Several weeks come and go. Mrs. Clark visits Jimmy daily at work and enjoys teaching him about Jesus. She gives him a Bible. Jimmy loves reading it. He has a Father in heaven who will never leave him. He learned to pray to God. He prayed from his heart and told God all about his problems. Jimmy always felt better after praying.

Mrs. Clark invited Jimmy to church this Sunday. She picked him up at the burger shop parking lot, and they drove to church. Jimmy got to hear the Word of God in church for the first time. He couldn't get over how the praise songs touched his heart. Jimmy learned that his Father in heaven loves him unconditionally—no matter what! And he learned that God desires to give him a hope and a future.

Jimmy goes to church every Sunday with Mrs. Clark. Today, he prayed the sinner's prayer and asked Jesus into his heart. In celebration of accepting Jesus as his Savior, he had lunch with Mrs. Clark. Her house was beautiful and smelled so nice. It was huge. Jimmy ate the best meal ever.

"Jimmy, you like my house?" she asked.

"Oh, sure. It's real nice."

She continued, "Jimmy, I would love for you to live here with me. Look, this could be your room.

You could walk back and forth to work. It would be great. I could use the company."

Jimmy paused. "No, I couldn't do that. It wouldn't be right."

"Oh, sure it would. I believe Jesus wants you to. He doesn't think you should be living under a bridge."

Jimmy couldn't believe she knew about that. He answered, "I'd love to."

"Great, Jimmy! Here's your room, some clothes, and this will be your bathroom. Just help yourself to anything in the kitchen you want," she replied.

Jimmy was overwhelmed.

Jimmy stayed there that night, and every night since. He was warm and safe at Mrs. Clark's house. Jimmy continued to work and saved all his money. He got his GED and eventually earned his college degree.

God is so good, he thought. He began thanking God daily for all the blessings God had given him. He prayed for Mrs. Clark and especially for his dad.

There was a girl at church that he liked, but was too nervous to talk to. Eventually he sat beside her. He didn't even know her name, but it was Molly.

Molly smiled at him and said, "It's about time you came and sat by me. My name is Molly. Jimmy, would you want to go eat lunch with me today after church?"

Jimmy said, "Sure." He wondered how she knew his name.

Eventually, they fell in love and got married. Two years later, they had one bad little boy named "Johnny."

A father of the fatherless and a judge for the widows, is God in His holy habitation.

Psalm 68:5 NASB

20.

Someone *Must* Punish Little Johnny!

Jimmy and Molly couldn't be happier. They had a new baby boy, Johnny. He was so cute. Jimmy couldn't believe how much he loved Little Johnny. He couldn't understand how anyone could mistreat a child. In time, Little Johnny welcomed his new baby sister, Julie. Johnny was sweet to Julie. He kissed her a lot. Johnny would say pee-yew when Julie had a dirty diaper.

Johnny and Julie played together all the time. Soon, they became best friends. When Johnny turned six, he got a puppy for his birthday and named him Jack. Johnny's favorite book was *Jack and the Beanstalk*. Jack was the perfect puppy, and he liked Julie, too.

A few years went by, and Johnny decided he didn't have to obey his parents anymore. He stopped doing his chores. He didn't care about doing well in school. Mr. Jimmy couldn't be mean to Johnny; he loved him too much. Mr. Jimmy would firmly tell Johnny he must do better. Johnny always smiled and said, "Sure, Dad, I'll do better," but Johnny never did. He got worse. Johnny thought it was great; he could do whatever he wanted, whenever he wanted. He knew he wasn't going to be punished.

Mr. Jones didn't like Johnny misbehaving, but he couldn't spank precious Little Johnny Boy. He didn't want Johnny to be mad at him or hate him. Johnny was getting way out of control, and it was breaking his dad's heart. Johnny's parents prayed and prayed that Jesus would fix things.

In church, Mr. Jimmy prayed for his family and for wisdom in rearing his children. The sermon was on "spare the rod and spoil the child." It means that you hate your son if you let him get away with acting badly. But, if you love your son, you will discipline him. Mr. Jimmy thought long and hard about that. That is what God was trying to teach him. Today, things are going to change. Poor Johnny doesn't know what's coming.

Now, when Johnny misbehaved, Mr. Jimmy punished him. Sometimes Mr. Jimmy took away Johnny's Xbox or wouldn't let him go outside to play with his friends. Johnny didn't like being punished. He thought, *Boy, what's going on?*

Johnny asked his dad why he got so mean all of a sudden. Mr. Jimmy asked, "Son, did you listen to the preacher Sunday? God says if I love you, and I do, that I will discipline you. If I don't discipline you, then I hate you. I don't hate you, Son. We have to obey God's Word. Faith is what gets us through tough times.

"God wanted Abraham's 'whole heart,' and He got it. Abraham would have sacrificed his only child, Isaac, if God hadn't stopped him at the last second. Isaac had tremendous faith too, because he obeyed his father. It was Abraham's faith in God that gave him the power to trust God. God blessed Abraham immensely.

"We are to obey. Period."

Johnny understood and said, "But that's so hard, Dad."

Mr. Jimmy replied, "Yes, it is at first. But the more we talk to God, the more we read His Word, and the more we remind God of His Word, the more faith we will have in Him. Think what you can do, Johnny, if you make God your very best friend forever!"

He who withholds his rod hates his son, but he who loves him disciplines him diligently.

Proverbs 13:24 NASB

21.

No, No! Not Johnny Boy!

We live on a dead-end street in a small town in Louisiana, four doors down from my grandparents. Most of the people that live here are related. If they aren't related, they are very close friends. Everyone knows what's going on down the street from day to day. There are no secrets here. Seems like my parents know what I've done before I've actually done it.

Once, I knocked over a trash can with my bike. I stopped and picked it up. I arrived at home five minutes later and Mom asked if I hurt myself when I hit the trash can. Can you believe that?

We all watch out for each other.

I'm ten now, and Julie is almost eight. It's Saturday morning. As soon as I finish my chores, I'm going to ride my bike. All of our neighbors spend a lot of time outside on the weekends. Kids ride bikes, skateboards and scooters. Old people walk for exercise and carry a big stick in case the neighbor's dog gets out. I always see two or three adults together talking. They are either catching up on gossip or talking about boiling crawfish.

I have cousins and close friends that live nearby. Their names are Westin, Bradley, Collin and Dwain. Westin's little sister, Jaidyn, is always hanging around, too. She's tough. She's always on her bike. When we play chase, I pick her to be on my team. It's unbelievable how fast she can move those legs of hers! She outruns all the guys.

Today I asked Westin, Bradley, Collin and Dwain if they wanted to go on an adventure with me. I made sure Jaidyn wasn't around. I didn't want anyone else to hear me. I knew she would tell her mom and dad if she knew what I was up to. She's a good kid. I told my buddies I wanted to sneak out of the house and spray-paint houses tonight. I asked them to come along. All of them, especially Westin, said no. They said, "You can't do that, it's wrong. If you get caught, it won't be pretty." After they said all of that, I told them I was just joking. I would never do such a thing.

That night, after supper, I put on a black long-sleeved shirt and black sweat pants and black tennis shoes and climbed into bed. When I was sure everyone was sound asleep, I snuck out of the house and went to the shed. I got an old can of orange spray paint. I was going to have fun.

I crossed the street to the other side. It was very dark out. I think this is Mr. Boudreaux's shed. I sprayed my orange paint all along the side of it as high as I could reach. I wanted to laugh, but I mustn't make any noise. I couldn't get caught. I ran a bit and sprayed another building, and then another, and then another. Wow!

Suddenly, a dog started barking. I took off running straight for home. I put the spray paint up and quietly slipped into bed. I didn't get caught. I was on cloud nine.

* * * * *

Early the next morning, everyone was getting ready for church. Mr. Landry was the first to go outside. He had orange paint sprayed on his house and was furious. He walked down the street a stretch and saw orange paint on other buildings. "We've been vandalized!" he yelled. Then Mr. Green and Mr. Allen came outside to look. It looked like a swarm of ants exiting houses and meeting in the middle of the street.

Someone asked, "Who would do such a thing?

Johnny chimed in, "Yeah! who would do that? That's awful."

Westin was standing right beside him. Westin thought Johnny probably did it. He certainly didn't want to accuse Johnny of wrongdoing without proof.

Johnny was laughing on the inside. He thought it was cool tricking all these people. Then he realized he sprayed his grandparents' house. Johnny wasn't sure how that happened.

Johnny's mom was mad when she saw that her parents' house had been vandalized. Mr. Jones told everyone to load up. He complained on the way to church about how he was going to have to repair Johnny's grandparents' house. Nothing is funny now.

* * * * *

At church, Johnny told his best friend, Bradley, what he had done. He asked Bradley to go with him tonight and spray-paint more houses. Bradley was shocked! He said no, and he was going to tell his dad. He was mad at Johnny, really mad.

Johnny told Bradly he couldn't tattle on him because they were friends. Johnny said, "You're not a snitch. Are you?" Bradley went home, and he didn't tell his dad what Johnny was up to.

After supper, Johnny showered and went to bed. In the middle of the night, he got up, went out, and painted three houses. At two o'clock in the morning, Mrs. Anna heard something and turned her front porch light on. She called her neighbor, who turned on her porch light, and she called her neighbor and so on. In no time at all, everyone was out on the porch and hollering, "Who are you? Why are you doing this? We are going to catch you!" Johnny was shaking in his shoes. He was trying to get home quickly.

The next morning, the neighbors gathered and couldn't stop talking about the rotten kid that vandalized their houses last night. Two of those houses had security cameras. Mr. Martinez reviewed the footage. There's the vandal, JOHNNY JONES! He's busted. Mr. Martinez found

Johnny's dad working a few doors down on his mother-in-law's house.

Mr. Jones was shocked to see Johnny in the video spray-painting a house. Mr. Jones told everyone that suffered damages that he would pay for all their repairs. No one gave him a hard time because they felt sorry for him.

Mr. Jones saw Johnny riding bikes with Bradley and Westin. He screamed, "JOHNNY, COME HERE NOW!" Johnny quickly headed straight to his dad.

Westin asked, "Bradley, did Johnny do it?"

"Yeah, I think so," answered Bradley.

Johnny asked, "What's wrong, Dad?"

Mr. Jones growled, "Johnny, get home right now. We have to talk."

When they got home, Johnny said, "It really wasn't me, Dad."

"You are on the security cameras. Johnny, how could you? I'm disappointed. You know better. Why would you do this?"

Johnny watched the video and hung his head. He answered, "I don't know. I'm really sorry for painting those houses."

"Tell me this, Son: Why in the heck did you paint your own grandparents' house?"

Johnny had no answer.

"Johnny, you are going to work and pay for everyone's repairs. I don't care if you have to work all summer. I don't care if you miss camping at Yogi Bear's Jellystone Park next month. Do you understand?" he asked.

"Yes sir," Johnny answered.

The next day, Johnny started at the front of the street and apologized to everyone involved. He told them he was going to pay for all the repairs. You could tell by the way they looked at Johnny that they were very disappointed in him. Some just shook their heads back and forth when they saw him. Mr. Cooper slammed the door in Johnny's face. Johnny knocked again, but this time harder. Mr. Cooper opened the door the second time. Johnny apologized and said he would pay for the repairs. Mr. Cooper yelled, "Good!" and slammed the door again.

Johnny got jobs cutting lawns. He sacked and carried out groceries in the evening at the local grocery. Mr. Boone hired Johnny to clean out his attic and garage. Johnny worked all that day and had no lunch. It was very hot, and he was hungry and exhausted. Mr. Boone took a lunch break and went inside. After eating lunch and taking about an hour nap, he went out to check on Johnny. At seven o'clock that night, Johnny stopped. He was finished. There was nothing more to be done. Mr. Boone said, "Son, I'm proud of you. You worked very hard and earned this money." He paid Johnny $200.

Johnny got a calculator and totaled up the cost of everyone's repairs. It came to $1,027.63. Word got around that Johnny was a strong, hard worker. More people hired him to clean out garages and shops and barns. He cut grass first thing in the morning, then cleaned out buildings, and every evening sacked groceries. He put every penny he earned in an envelope. The envelope was getting fat.

Seven weeks later, Johnny counted the money he kept in the envelope. He had $1,000. He had one week to make $27.63, and he knew he could earn that. Johnny was proud of himself. He hoped Dad would let him go camping at Yogi even though he didn't deserve it.

He told God, "Thank You for giving me these jobs and helping me fix all that I did wrong. Thank You loving me when I'm unlovable. I'm sorry I spray-painted all those buildings. Forgive me. Help me be a good son to Dad and to You. Amen."

Two days later, Johnny gave his dad the full $1,027.63. Mr. Jones was pleased that Johnny worked hard and earned the money to pay off his debt. Mr. Jones' neighbors called earlier and told him what a fine job Johnny had done working for them. They expressed that they forgave Johnny and that he was still welcomed at their house. The neighbors insisted Johnny had learned his lesson.

Johnny's dad said, "I've been praying for you, Son. I hope you've learned your lesson."

"Oh, I have, Dad. Honestly, I have," he insisted.

Mr. Jones told Johnny he could go to Yogi.

Johnny screamed, "Thank You, Lord JESUS!"

"For nothing is hidden that will not become evident, nor anything secret that will not be known and come to light."

Luke 8:17 NASB

22.

The Horrible, Awful Scream: "Dad!"

Johnny and his dad were going craw-fishing this fine Saturday morning at the Bonnet Carre spillway. The spillway is an area used for overflow of the river. The gates had been opened to lower the river water level and help reduce the chance of flooding downstream. The spillway had been opened for a couple of weeks. The waterway is completely flooded between the Mississippi River and Lake Pontchartrain. It was a beautiful site to see.

The water rages through the opened gates with lightning speed. It rips through the spillway and empties into Lake Pontchartrain. It looks like danger-ous rolling white rapids. There's a frenzy of bird activity. Pelicans and seagulls are diving into the water for a feast. Large bald eagles take part catching an easy meal as well. They are instantly spotted with those beautiful white heads.

The spillway has now been closed. The water had risen to twelve feet. It takes days to drain into Lake Pontchartrain. The water level is finally down low enough so we can go crawfishing. Dad loaded everything up and we headed to the spillway. We were meeting my cousin Ethan and his family there. The plan was to catch sacks and sacks of crawfish. I love boiled crawfish. Dad loves crawfish étouffée. Memaw loves crawfish fettuc-cine. We're going to fish all day long. Dad even brought a big pot to boil craw-fish right there by our truck for lunch. Talk about good! I don't suck the heads, but baby girl Julie sure does. She's a mess.

We arrive. There are people everywhere. They already have their nets set. You could see areas of all red flags, all yellow flags, and some checkered flags. Our nets are purple and gold of course. We're huge LSU tiger fans, and we bleed purple and gold. Our nets are now set, and we are crawfishing.

Oh, here comes little Ethan hiking in his red rubber boots. Uncle Simon is leading the way down. Ethan, four years old, is following him, and Alli is following Ethan. Alli, short for Allison, is eight years old. Aunt Liz is still gathering things from the truck. Uncle Simon is telling them, "Follow me. Be careful. Stay close."

You see, there are a lot of culverts under the dirt roads in the spillway. You can't see them. There's still plenty of water rushing around dirt mounds. Deep ponds everywhere continue to drain underground. The moving water shoots through a maze of culverts and out to the lake. The ground is unlevel.

Uncle Simon said, "Stay on high ground, guys. Watch your step." I could hear them, but I wasn't watching them. I was busy helping Dad lift our nets. We had crawfish all over the place. We had never caught so many crawfish so fast. *Memaw is going to love this,* I thought.

Suddenly, I heard this horrible, awful, scream. "DAD!!!"

I got goose bumps. Who could be screaming? Why is she screaming? I looked around. I saw Alli.

She was hysterical. She's screaming uncontrollably over and over, "It's Ethan, he's gone!" Uncle Simon dropped everything and turned around. In a flash, Ethan had vanished.

Aunt Liz screamed, "My baby! Simon, find him!"

People swarmed into the area. Everybody was bobbing up and down in the ponds trying to find Ethan, even me. I could feel the current try to pull my watch off. My shirt was pulled against my neck ever so tightly. The water didn't look that swift, but it was.

Alli was too upset and too small to help. She kept saying, "Please save my brother."

A stranger nearby called the cops. The cops arrived and called for an ambulance. It looked hopeless. No one can survive staying underwater that long. Uncle Simon turned pale white. He was frantically running, diving, reaching, and absolutely nonstop praying, "God help me. I have to find Ethan."

An ambulance arrived on the scene. It had been a long time since Ethan went under the water. People around us started crying. They believed Ethan had drowned, but not his mom. She never stopped praying. She told God she didn't care how bad the situation appeared; she knew He was God. She said, "You are the Miracle Maker. You gave me my son, and I haven't finished raising him. God, I trust You. You are my Help. You are my Hope. I want to see the victory, NOW. I need it NOW, dear God."

At that very moment, Uncle Simon saw one of Ethan's little red boots pop up out of the water a few feet away. As it floated off, Uncle Simon ran with all his might to get to the spot where it came up. Water was up to his hips. He had to fight hard to free his feet from the thick, gooey mud that closed in on them with each step. He reached the spot. "Dear God, help me. Where's Ethan?"

Under the water Uncle Simon went. He felt around. He felt a culvert. He reached in. He felt something like a foot, but couldn't get a grip. He was out of air. Uncle Simon quickly came up, took a deep breath and frantically went under again. His head was underwater, but his feet were kicking something awful above the water. He reached in the culvert. He felt a leg. He knew it was Ethan's leg. This was the most scared Uncle Simon had ever been in his life. *What if…?* he thought. He ripped Ethan right out of that culvert.

Ethan was alive! He wasn't even crying. He said, "Daddy, I was in a tunnel going really fast. I was going this way and then that way. I couldn't get out." Ethan didn't have a scratch on him.

Aunt Liz started praising God and ran to grab Ethan. She prayed, "Thank You for this miracle. Thank You for Your blessings." She snatched Ethan up and loved on him. Aunt Liz got into the ambulance with the paramedics and rode with Ethan to the hospital to be checked out.

When the ambulance pulled out and turned on the sirens, poor Uncle Simon collapsed. His legs just gave out. He realized that God had just performed a miracle for him, for his family. He was overwhelmed with gratitude.

I was standing by Uncle Simon and Alli. I patted his shoulder and said, "God is good, huh?"

Memaw and Pawpaw didn't go crawfishing. They met Ethan at the hospital. He was fine and got to go home. Boy, will Memaw have a praise report for Sunday school tomorrow. She sure likes to brag on God.*

I lift up my eyes to the mountains-where does my help come from? My help comes from the LORD, the Maker of heaven and earth.

Psalm 121:1–2 NIV

23.

Mr. Burns' Buddies

Mr. Burns is outside this morning, so Johnny heads over for a visit. Sitting on the swing, Johnny asked, "Mr. Burns, do you have any good stories for me?"

"Well," said Mr. Burns, "I do have one that's happy and sad, but mostly happy. I don't know if you want to hear it."

"I do, but I want it all to be good, Mr. Burns. Just make it up," said Johnny.

"No, Johnny. I can't do that. It's important. I think you're big enough to hear it. This is a true story."

"Yeah, I'm big. Tell me," Johnny insisted.

* * * * *

When I was young, I had a good friend named Chuck. We were the same age. We climbed trees, crawfished, and went hunting and fishing together. We went swimming all summer. Every June, his mom took us to Vacation Bible School for the week. We were both saved at VBS before we turned ten. Our parents were so happy. Chuck and I were nearly inseparable.

We had another friend named Doug. Chuck hung out with him more than I did because Doug lived close to Chuck's house. Chuck and I did well in school. Doug kind of struggled. He made mostly Cs and Ds. His dad was always on him to make better grades.

Chuck would say, "Gee, Doug, you need to pray. Jesus says, if we don't have wisdom, just ask for it. He will give it to you." We both told him that we pray for wisdom all the time. Doug always said no. For some reason, Doug got mad when we offered to help him. We never understood why he would say no to prayer.

After graduation, Chuck enrolled at Tulane University and got a part-time job at the gas station. Doug enrolled at Tulane as well and got a job at a hamburger place. The buddies shared an apartment with two other students. All the guys got along well. Doug wasn't passing his classes and still refused to pray about it. Doug wouldn't pray about anything.

* * * * *

"Why wouldn't he, Mr. Burns?" asked Johnny. "Everybody needs help, and Jesus can help. I ask Jesus to help me all the time."

"I really don't know why he wouldn't, Johnny. Chuck and I could never figure it out. Sad, isn't it?"

* * * * *

Doug dropped out of college and started working full-time as a cook at the hamburger joint. He made very little money. Chuck, on the other hand, graduated from Tulane with an engineering degree and got a great job. Eventually, he met Esther, and they got married. Doug attended their wedding. I think he was jealous that Chuck landed a job that paid so well and married a sweet girl.

Two years later, Chuck had a baby boy. He excitedly called Doug and told him about Baby Boy Corbin. He even invited him to church Sunday for Baby Dedication Day. Doug refused; he didn't want to go. Two years later, Chuck had twin girls.

Chuck put God first in all areas of his life. His family regularly prayed together. Chuck wanted his children to know that God is a jealous God. He must come first in their lives. God richly blessed Chuck and his family over the years.

Chuck and Doug lived very different lives. As time passed, the buddies grew far, far apart. One day, Doug's sister,

Bonnie, called Chuck. She told Chuck that poor Doug was in the hospital and very ill. She had stayed day and night with him all week. "He asked about you, Chuck. I know y'all were once close. He wants to see you," she pleaded.

Chuck answered, "Sure, where is he?"

Bonnie gave Chuck all the hospital information.

Doug was lying in a hospital bed when Chuck walked into his room. Doug looked gravely ill. Chuck almost cried when he saw him. Doug was extremely weak, but he did ask Chuck to pray for him. Chuck prayed. He then asked Doug if he could share the gospel with him, and Doug weakly said yes.

Chuck asked Doug if he was a sinner and if he was sorry for his sins. Doug nodded yes. Chuck asked if he believed Jesus Christ was the son of God and died for his sins. Doug softly and slowly answered yes. Chuck then asked Doug if he wanted Jesus to live in his heart and accept him as his Savior. Doug smiled, and with a bit more strength, answered yes. It was an emotional conversation. Doug cried because for the first time, he realized that Jesus truly loved him beyond measure. Jesus loved him so much that He died on the cross for him. Jesus died for Doug, and you, and me and everyone. And Chuck cried because he was thrilled that he will spend all eternity with his friend one day.

* * * * *

"Yeah, now that's something to get excited about, isn't it Mr. Burns?" asked Johnny.

Mr. Burns announced, "That's the most important decision anyone will ever make."

Johnny agreed. "Oh, I know that, Mr. Burns. Anyone that's saved knows that. Our lives on earth are short even if we live to be a hundred, but eternity, that's forever and ever."

Doug passed away just minutes after accepting Jesus Christ as his Savior. Chuck was right at his side. Chuck was sad and happy at the same time. It doesn't matter if Doug was saved at ten years old, or a hundred and ten years old. He's still in heaven with Jesus. And I will see him there one day, too.

"But Mr. Burns, it's sad Doug didn't have as good a life as you and Chuck. If only he had accepted Jesus sooner and prayed to Him. He sure missed out on blessings, on so many blessings, didn't he?" Johnny asked.

"He sure did, Johnny," Mr. Burns replied.

And He said to him, "Truly I say to you, today you shall be with Me in Paradise."

Luke 23:43 NASB

24.

That Poor, Poor Man Is Nearly Dead

Johnny's dad said, "Sit here, next to me, Johnny." Baby Girl Julie always sits next to their mom. The pastor began preaching. Sometimes he yelled, sometimes he spoke softly, and sometimes they saw him cry. Sometimes Johnny listened, sometimes he didn't.

Today, the pastor told the old story about the Good Samaritan. There was this poor fellow who got beaten up by someone and left for dead on the dirt road. Several people saw him. They heard him whimpering and moaning at a distance. Did any of them go help him? NO! They all walked way, way around him. Johnny thought to himself, *Jesus can't be happy about that. He would have helped this poor, hurt man.*

Pastor said a Samaritan came by and ran to the man when he saw him lying on the ground and heard him moaning. Buzzards were circling in the sky just above him. The Samaritan picked his head up off the burning sand. He wiped blood off the poor man's face and told him, "I've got you. You are going to be all right." Then the Samaritan gave the poor man a drink of water. The weak man was so badly hurt that he could hardly move. He couldn't hold his head up for long and didn't have the strength to hold the water skin to take a drink.

People continued walking by, but still, they kept their distance and didn't offer to help. Only the Samaritan felt compassion for him. Johnny thought that was sad, and he's just a kid; those people were grown-ups.

The Good Samaritan picked the man up and lugged him into town. He prayed to God, "Please give me Your strength and help me carry him to safety. I know he's Your child too, and You love him." The Samaritan found a place for him to stay and people who would take care of him. The Good Samaritan paid the people to give him a bath; to give him food and medicine; and to let him stay there long enough to heal. The Samaritan said he would pay more when he returned, if it cost more.

Soon, the poor man felt a lot better and healed. Somebody actually cared enough not to leave him on the hot blazing dirt road to die and become food for wild animals. The Samaritan was a nice man. He chose to love and care for someone he had never met simply because he knew God loved him.

Johnny thought about that story for days.

* * * * *

There was an incident during recess at school this week. Some of Johnny's friends were being mean to the new kid, Paul. Paul had just moved here two weeks ago. He hadn't really made friends yet. Paul seemed like an okay guy. Johnny thought, *What would Jesus want me to do?* He marched up to those boys and said, "Stop that! Don't be mean to Paul. He's my friend."

Some kid yelled, "Well, if he's your friend, then you're not our friend anymore!"

Johnny said, "Fine with me."

All of Johnny's friends ran off. Paul was the only boy left standing there.

Paul was confused. He asked, "Do I know you? I just moved here. Nobody is my friend."

Johnny smiled and said, "Well, I'm your new best friend then, Paul. We're going to be great pals."

Paul thought that was weird, but it made him happy. Johnny and Paul ran to the swings and swung. They ran to the slides and slid. Then they played chase.

Paul runs much faster than Johnny. Johnny really didn't like that.

When Johnny walked home, he thought about the day. He lost friends, but he made a new friend. He believed Jesus was happy that he defended Paul. He bet his dad would be proud of him, too. He was going to run and meet Dad when he got home from work and tell him what had happened. *Today, Julie won't have the only good story to tell.*

Johnny did just that. He told his dad about taking up for the new kid. Dad was very proud of Johnny. At dinner, Johnny took great delight in telling his mom all that had happened. She almost cried and said, "Oh Johnny. That is the sweetest thing. You be sure to invite Paul over to play sometime. I am proud of you."

That night, when Johnny went to bed, he talked to Jesus about Paul. Johnny was super glad he listened to the preacher Sunday. "Jesus, You know it's a mean world here sometimes, but I'm glad You made good kids like Paul to be my friend. I'm going to invite him over this weekend to meet Jack and ride bikes. Please don't let the kids in the neighborhood be mean to us. Amen."

* * * * *

Saturday morning, Paul arrived at Johnny's house. He was so excited. Paul pedaled his bike and towed his skateboard tied to his bike. He was ready for the day. Paul got to meet Jack, Johnny's dog. Jack jumped up and gave Paul a wet slobbery kiss. Johnny said, "I knew he was going to like you. He's never done that to any of my other friends." They laughed so hard that Jack got excited and started barking and jumping around. Jack is the best pet of all time.

Soon thereafter, kids from the neighborhood showed up. Some were riding bikes, scooters, skateboards and pogo sticks. The mean one, Will, actually smiled and said, "Hey, y'all want to follow us to the park. We're going to play all day."

Johnny asked Paul, "What do you think?"

Paul was all smiles. "You bet. Let's go!"

They all went to the park and played chase. Johnny noticed a little girl about their age, crying by the swings. Several bigger boys were standing around her and calling her names.

Johnny called all his buddies into a huddle. "What are we going to do about this?" he asked. "She's a girl, and they shouldn't be ugly to her. They are much bigger than we are. If we interfere, they might start a fight. Are we ready to fight bigger guys?"

Paul jumped up. "You bet. If God is for us, who can be against us?"

Then Will stood up and said, "YEAH. LET'S GO GET THE GIRL!"

And so they did. They told those boys, "Get out of here. Stop being mean to her, or you'll have us to deal with. And you don't want that!"

No one fought. The bullies just walked away. Her name is Alleigh. She can out-run everyone except Paul. Johnny thinks she's cool!

Johnny prayed silently, *Thank You for my new friend Alleigh. Amen.*

"You shall love your neighbor as yourself; I am the LORD."

Leviticus 19:18 NASB

25.

All the Kids Have Rudolph Noses

I slept all night. Mom came in this morning and woke me. She said, "Get up and get dressed. I don't want you to miss the bus again." So, I got up, got dressed, and went to the kitchen to eat breakfast. There was Julie, all spiffy, bow in her hair, shoes shined, nail polish all perfect, smiling big with huge white teeth. Sickening.

The bus came. Julie had eaten her pancakes, mine were on the table. Julie and I had to run out to catch the bus. Mom smiled and said, "I guess I get pancakes this morning."

School was the same today as it was yesterday. When I went to reading class, I said, "Jesus please help me do well in reading. Amen."

Mrs. Smith told us to get out our reading books, and she picked me to read a whole chapter in front of the class. I wish she hadn't done that. *Dear Jesus, please help me,* I prayed silently.

I walked to the front of the class with my book. My hands were sweating and my legs got weak. All the kids were staring at me. I was scared. *Dear Jesus, please help.*

I started reading. I made a mistake and heard Dennis chuckle. I paused a minute. Then I started again. It was going pretty well. It was an exciting story. I screamed when I saw exclamation marks, and I talked softly when it indicated someone was whispering. I didn't even look at the kids in my class. I was into this story. It was awesome!

The chapter was about a guy named Jonah. God had told him to go to Nineveh. Jonah wasn't about to go to Nineveh, so he boarded a ship to go the opposite way. A violent storm came up very suddenly. There was lightning and thunder. The waves grew taller than a two-story building. Everything was rocking and bouncing about. The ship took on water and sank. Jonah was trying to stay afloat, but he could fight the waves no longer.

He knew this was the end. He gasped for his last breath and was going to drown. In a flash, a whale jumped out of the water and came down over Jonah and swallowed him whole.

Jonah was in the belly of the whale with nasty, smelly, gooey, slimy yuk. It was pitch-dark inside the whale's stomach. Jonah could feel something moving in the gooey yuk but couldn't see it. The gurgling sounds worried him. He was afraid. For three whole days, Jonah smelled the awful smell and sat in slime. He threw up a lot. It was disgusting. Jonah prayed and wished he had obeyed God and went to Nineveh as God instructed him.

On the third day, the whale spit Jonah out onto the shore. Jonah gleefully ran back into the water and washed off! He prayed, "Thank You, God, for allowing the whale to swallow me and save my life." Jonah ate lunch and then traveled straight to Nineveh as God had told him.

That ended the story. When Johnny looked up, all the kids were glued to him. They began saying, "Tell us more. More, Johnny. Make it longer."

Johnny smiled and said, "Read your Bible, Bro."

The kids started clapping. Johnny could tell Mrs. Smith was proud of him. "Johnny, you did a fine job," she said.

Johnny thought, *From now on, when I'm scared, hurt, or mad, I'm going to pray to Jesus for help. He always makes things better. I can't believe I did that well. Reading isn't so bad.*

Paul, Johnny's best friend, came over and asked, "Johnny, how did you do that? I don't like talking to a bunch of people, I could never read in front a class."

"Sure, you could, Paul. Just pretend everybody out there has a big fat red blinking nose like Rudolph. Then you can't help but laugh. It takes the edge off."

"Is that what you did?"

Johnny shook his head. "No. I didn't. I did something so much better."

"What was that?" Paul asked.

"I prayed to the Lord Jesus Christ. He can do anything, and He says I can do anything through Him. I believe Him."

I sought the LORD, and He answered me, and delivered me from all my fears.

Psalm 34:4 NASB

I can do all things through Him who strengthens me.

Philippians 4:13 NASB

26.

My Report Card, I Can't Look

I'm Johnny, and I'm twelve years old. My sister, Julie, is ten years old. I don't like Julie because she is so **perfect**. It's sickening. She does everything right all the time and never gets in trouble. Julie is always polite and answers "yes ma'am" and "no ma'am." It's disgusting to see Mom and Dad smile at her all the time because she does well in school. They say, "Oh Julie, I'm so proud of you. Keep up the good work, dear." It makes my stomach turn.

I don't make good grades. I hate school. Dad always tells me to do my best. He would say, "If you do well in school, you can get a good job and take care of a family someday. Don't you want to have your own place one day?

You want to go on vacations? Go hunting?"

Of course, I do, but I'm not going to tell him that. Reading is my worst subject. Why do you need so much of that anyway?

I'm worried. Report cards come out in a week. Dad said I have to make at least a C in reading for the year or I won't be going to Yogi Bear's Jellystone Park this summer. We are having a family reunion there. All my aunts, uncles, cousins and grandparents will be there.

My reading teacher, Mrs. Smith, begins handing out our report cards.

Please, please, please let it be a C or better. Dad's not going to be happy if it's not. My hands are sweating. I must go

to Yogi Bear this summer. Please, please, please.

Mrs. Smith handed me my report card, and she wasn't smiling like she did when she gave everybody else their report card. That's not a good sign.

Oh no, it's a D! What am I going to do?

I walked home slowly.

Julie said, "Come on, Johnny. I can't wait to show Dad my report card. I got all As. He's going to be so proud of me."

I walked even slower. *Dad is not going to be proud of me.*

Oh great, Dad's home. There goes Julie running out the door, screaming, "Daddy, Daddy! Look, all As. Are you proud of me?" Of course, he is.

Dinner smells delicious. I wish I felt like eating. Dad's going to ask about my report card. Did I mention that I hate school?

"Johnny, come on down. It's time to eat," yelled Dad.

"Hi, Dad, how was your day?" I asked.

"Fine, Son, just fine. Now, I'm dying to hear about your report card. Please tell me you did well."

I couldn't look at Dad. My head was hanging down. "I- I- I..." I tried to answer but couldn't find the words. Finally, I blurted out, "I made a D. I didn't try hard enough. I don't like school."

Julie said, "I love school, Daddy!"

Dad told me he agreed. He knew I could do the work, but I didn't try hard enough. He reminded me I had six weeks to figure it out and pass with a C. He explained that an education is important and there are consequences for not working hard enough.

* * * * *

Johnny began paying attention in class. He read everything twice. He studied at home. Johnny even asked Jesus for wisdom every day at school and every night before bed. He wanted Dad to be proud of him, too. He doesn't really hate Julie. He's glad she does well, he just wished he did better.

It's the last day of school. Mrs. Smith is passing out final report cards. Johnny is very nervous. His heart is pounding. Mrs. Smith was not smiling when she handed Johnny his report card. He wanted to look at the grade, he tried to look at his grade, but he just couldn't. Johnny must make a C. Finally, Johnny looked: a C. He began screaming on the inside.

Hip hip hooray! I made a C. I'm going to Yogi Bear. CHICK A CHICK A BOOM BOOM, BABY. CHICK A CHICK A BOOM BOOM! Whoa, I did it. It really wasn't so bad. Jesus is so good. He can help anybody do anything and I'm proof of that. Wait until I see my Memaw. She's going to be proud of me, too.

"Dear Jesus. Thank You so much. Thank You, thank you, thank you. Amen."

But if any of you lacks wisdom, let him ask of God, who gives to all generously and without reproach, and it will be given to him.

James 1:5 NASB

27.

Paul Can't Kick a Soccer Ball

All the kids are going to the park this Saturday morning. We are going to play all day. I can't wait to see Paul. He's cool. Now all my old friends are friends with Paul. We started out playing baseball and that got old. Everyone decided to take a break under the huge moss-covered oak tree nearby. It was breezy and cool in the shade. I could hear the wind blow through the branches. Boy, did that feel good. I wondered how God made beautiful trees like this one.

Out of the blue, Will said, "Okay, enough baseball. I've been wanting to play soccer. Let's play soccer. I brought my soccer ball."

All the kids discussed it a few minutes and decided to play soccer.

Paul didn't like the idea. He told me he couldn't play soccer. Paul didn't want to lose his friends over a game of soccer. I told Paul not to worry, it would be all right. Will said, "OK, everybody, let's have a few warm up plays, then we'll pick teams." Paul was nervous.

One kid kicked the ball to another, he kicked it to someone else, and that kid kicked it into the goal. Some of the kids jumped up and down and high-fived each other. The other kids were complaining. One said, "You were supposed to intercept the ball." Another said, "Why didn't you stop the ball from going into the goal?" and so on.

Will said, "All right everybody, line up. It's time for us to pick teams. Since Johnny and Tim picked teams for baseball, me and Evan are picking teams for soccer."

Will picked Johnny first. Then Evan picked someone to be on his team. Guess who got picked last? Yep, Paul was picked dead last. Johnny didn't like that, but someone is always picked first, and someone is always picked last.

The game began. It started out slowly. The kids were being cautious. Each team was figuring out their plays, and what worked well for them. Everybody, that is, except Paul. The speed of the game really picked up. The ball was moving around so fast, it was hard to keep an eye on it.

Paul tried to kick the ball to his teammates several times. It was awful. Once, the ball went into the ditch. One time, Paul kicked it and it hit a five-year-old girl on the head. She was by the swings and started crying. The little girl's mom ran to her and made a mean face at Paul. Paul felt awful. Johnny could tell by the way he looked.

Paul has the shot. No one was near him. He concentrates. He's focused. Paul's tongue is pressed between his teeth. He prays, *Just let it go into the goal.*

Paul ran as fast as he could, he took aim, and he kicked. The ball was still in the same spot; it didn't move a bit. Paul missed the ball completely. He did a complete summersault in the air and landed flat on his back. It all happened in the blink of an eye. It's a wonder that the only thing that got hurt was Paul's feelings.

A few of the kids snickered. Some wanted to kick Paul off the team. Paul heard, "He can't play soccer. He's awful. He should just be a cheerleader and cheer for us like the girls do." Paul wanted to cry, but he didn't.

Everyone quit for the day and went home. They all agreed to pick teams tomorrow after church and play again.

Paul walked home with Johnny. "Have you ever played soccer before?" Johnny asked.

Paul answered, "No. Not really. I can't kick the ball good enough."

"That doesn't mean anything," Johnny replied.

"Of course, it does," Paul said.

"Nope, not at all. Come on. You ready to learn something? I'm going to teach you how to be the best goalie ever. You'll be on my team tomorrow," Johnny insisted.

Paul wished he was as confident as Johnny was.

The boys went into Johnny's backyard.

Johnny explained, "When you see the guy running to the ball, watch his leg line up on the ball. If he's coming from way out and then inward, line up inward. The ball will come that way. If the ball goes high in the air and two are running toward it, be careful because one might hit it with his head into the goal. In that case, be ready to jump and catch the ball. Let's practice. Watch me. Watch my face. You will be able to read which way I'm going to kick or hit the ball into the net. Line up accordingly."

"Okay, Johnny, I'm going to give it my best," Paul replied.

They prayed to Jesus for guidance and practiced for an hour. Both were tired, but they were having fun. Paul was playing better with each play.

Johnny was impressed how fast Paul was learning. *Tomorrow, Paul is going to be just fine,* he thought.

* * * * *

Everyone gathered at the park. Johnny and Tim began picking teams. Johnny picked Paul first! No one could believe it. Paul is awful. Johnny just smiled. They continued choosing teammates until the teams were created.

The soccer game began. Paul and Johnny had something to prove. They wanted everyone to see what could happen when you ask Jesus for help and practice. The game was close, but Paul had already blocked five "near" goals. He did let one get through. The score is tied 1–1.

Oh, but wait, yep, Johnny's team just scored again. It's now 2–1 with only one minute left in the game. Everyone is running fast. The ball is being kicked and hit about. It was changing directions constantly—a wild scene. Oh no, here comes Bradley!

Bradley's on Tim's team and he's their best kicker. He usually scores the most points.

Paul is nervous. Here goes nothing. He concentrates on Bradley's eyes. He can tell Bradley's going to kick the ball high and to the left side of the goal. Paul thought, *BRING IT ON BIG BOY. I'M READY FOR YOU. ALL RIGHT JESUS, LET'S DO THIS!*

Bradley runs. He kicks. Here comes the ball.

Paul jumps, hands up high. BAM! The ball hits Paul's hands, it ricochets. Does it go in the goal? NO!

Yeah! Johnny's team wins! Paul's a hero. He saved the game. "We win!" scream a couple of the kids. They run to Paul and pick him up and carry him on their shoulders around the field. They were all chanting, "Paul's our HERO!" Johnny was happy for Paul. Paul was thankful for his friend Johnny.

> *A friend loves at all times, and a brother is born for adversity.*
>
> Proverbs 17:17 NASB

28.

Old Fisherman

Mr. Burns is an old man who lives next door. He's almost eighty and still goes fishing several times a week. I like Mr. Burns. I cut his grass, and he pays me to do it. That gives me money to go to the movies with Nanan.

Mr. Burns lives with his dog, Trigger. He loves Trigger. Every evening Mr. Burns sits on his swing and watches Trigger play. My dog, Jack, chases Trigger around the house. They run fast and get hot.

Mr. Burns yells, "Turn on the hose pipe and cool them off, Johnny."

I think it's funny he calls the water hose a "hose pipe." It's fun to watch our dogs jump and lap at the water. Jack actually smiles when I spray him. Mr. Burns sits and shakes his head.

Today he said, "Hey, Johnny, you want a popsicle?"

"Sure, Mr. Burns," I answered.

"Great. Go get me a green one please, and you can get two. You're a growing boy!"

"Gee, thanks, Mr. Burns."

I went and got the popsicles. As we sat on the swing and ate popsicles, Mr. Burns asked if I would like to go fishing with him. He told me he was getting older, and it was getting harder for him to get the boat winched up on the trailer, to pull the anchor up, and to throw the cast net. I told him sure, but I would have to check with my parents first.

I asked, "Would it be okay if I brought along my best friend, Paul?"

"Sure, it would, Johnny," Mr. Burns answered.

I ran home and hollered, "Mom, Dad, can I go fishing with Mr. Burns tomorrow? He's having a lot of trouble pulling the boat up on the trailer, pulling the anchor up, and reeling in big fish. He needs me."

Mr. Jones answered, "I think that will be fine, Son, but you better mind Mr. Burns. He has to maintain control of the boat to keep you safe. Remember, he's the captain."

"Sure, Dad. I know. I know. Really, I know," I repeated. "I've got to call Paul. He said Paul could come, too." I called my friend. When he answered, I said, "Paul, ask your dad if you can come fishing with me and Mr. Burns tomorrow."

Paul started yelling for his mom and asked her if he could go.

She said yes, then added, "Behave yourself."

"Yeah, Johnny, I can go," he said.

"Be here at my house at 4:30 a.m.," I told him. "We'll walk over to Mr. Burns house at 5:00 a.m. Bring sunscreen and something to drink."

* * * * *

The next morning, the boys were so excited, they started beating on Mr. Burns' front door at 4:30 a.m. Mr. Burns was just pouring himself a cup of coffee. *Darn*, he thought, *they are early*. He opened the door. The kids were all smiles and had bags of stuff. "Whatcha got there, boys? he asked.

"Our drinks and snacks," they answered.

"I see. Well, let's go get it loaded," said Mr. Burns.

The boys couldn't stop asking questions. "Where can I sit? Where does this go? Where's the cooler for our drinks? Where is Paul going to sit? You have life jackets for us? Can I drive the boat?"

They had so much food. Mr. Burns couldn't see how two kids could eat all the food they were stashing in his boat. The boys talked about catching redfish and

croakers. One mentioned his mom likes speckled trout the best.

This was Paul's first fishing trip. Mr. Burns enjoyed watching the boys have a good time and seeing Paul catch his first fish. The boys had never had so much fun. This was all new to Mr. Burns.

Mr. Burns doesn't have children or grandchildren. He prayed, "Lord Jesus, thank You for such a wonderful day as today, to watch Your children enjoy Your creation. Please help me keep them safe. Amen."

The boys were pulling in fish left and right. Around 2:00 p.m., Mr. Burns headed back to the dock. Their ice chest was overloaded with fish!

Johnny helped Mr. Burns load the boat back onto the trailer. After Mr. Burns pulled the boat out of the water, Paul collected all their trash and threw it away. Johnny saw to it any lose objects in the boat were put away or tied down. After Mr. Burns made sure all the tie downs were snug, he started the truck and they headed home.

Johnny and Paul never stopped talking. They couldn't wait to tell their parents about the day. They caught 6 big redfish, 14 speckled trout, 22 white trout, 9 croakers, 5 flounder, 2 sheepshead and 1 Spanish mackerel. They caught a lot more, but they weren't keepers. Paul couldn't get over the teeth in the sheepshead mouth (they looked like human teeth). It was going to be a lot work to clean all those fish.

As soon as they got home, Johnny ran to his house screaming for his dad. "Dad, we caught a million fish, and Mr. Burns could use your help."

Mr. Jones called Paul's dad, and the two men helped Mr. Burns filet the fish. Bags of fish were divided up and given to each family. Mr. Jones invited Mr. Burns to a fish fry the next day after church. Mr. Burns said he would love to. "By the way, Mr. Burns, if you would like to go to church with us tomorrow, we love to take you."

"I believe I will, that sounds good," Mr. Burns replied.

Johnny's dad told him to be ready at 10:00 a.m.

* * * * *

Sunday morning, Johnny's family loaded in the car. Mr. Burns was sitting on his swing in his regular clothes. I guess that's all he has to wear. He looked good though; he looked like Mr. Burns. Jesus will like it no matter what he wears.

Johnny asked him to sit next to him, but Julie said, "No, I want him to sit by me."

Johnny insisted, "No, he's my friend. He's going to sit by me. Aren't you, Mr. Burns?"

Mr. Jones had to intervene. "Mr. Burns is our guest, and he's going to see up front with me."

Mrs. Jones told Julie to scoot over, and she sat in the back seat with Julie and Johnny. Mr. Burns couldn't stop smiling.

When they walked into church, Mr. Burns couldn't get over how pretty it was. The people were very nice. Only one lady looked at him like he should have dressed better, but he didn't care. He knew he was there to learn more about Jesus, not about impressing people.

Johnny didn't know it, but Mr. Burns reads his Bible every day. He probably knows as much about the Bible as anyone there. Mr. Burns particularly liked singing. Johnny watched him. He started off singing softly, but then he really got into it. He was singing praises louder that most of the people around them. Johnny liked that, and he knew Jesus liked it, too. Mr. Burns had rhythm too—he was tapping his toes, clapping his hands, and wiggling his butt. He was having a good time!

Johnny prayed, "Dear Jesus, thank You for my friend, Mr. Burns."

Let them praise His name with dancing; let them sing praises to Him with timbrel and lyre. For the LORD takes pleasure in His people.

Psalm 149:3–4 NASB

29.

Johnny Found a Wallet

All my friends have skateboards, but not me. I really want a skateboard. Sometimes, my friend George lets me ride his skateboard while he rides his bike. My bike's broken. Dad told me I had to buy my own skateboard and fix my bike. I can earn the money to buy a skateboard by doing chores, but I don't want to work.

Through my window, I see four of my friends outside riding their skateboards right now. Timmy's dad built a huge curved ramp. The kids run fast, throw their skateboard down on the ramp, and then jump on it. They ride to the other side of the board, thrust up into the air, flip in mid-air, free fall back to the ramp, and do it all over again. Everyone laughs when someone falls down. I want to buy a skateboard. I'm going start doing my chores now.

Skateboards cost about $50. If I do my chores every week, I'll have enough money to buy a skateboard by May. This will work out fine. I'll have a new skateboard before summer.

* * * * *

Johnny emptied all the trash cans and took out the trash. He cleaned his room and his bathroom. Then Johnny vacuumed all the carpets. Lastly, Johnny fed his dog, Jack, and then brushed his fur until it shined. He loves Jack, and Jack loves him. Johnny really didn't know why he got lazy at times and didn't take care of Jack. Jack always met Johnny in the yard after school, fetched the ball for him, and even followed Johnny everywhere he went.

All of Johnny's friends wished they had a dog like Jack. Bradley's dog bites people, so he must wear a muzzle. Jim's dog is named Porky because he looks like a piglet and steals everybody's food. Luke's dog is named Sergeant. Sarge sounds like he's dying when he barks, and he barks at everything, including mailboxes! But Jack, he's perfect. Seriously, he's the perfect pet.

Johnny did well in school today and didn't get any marks in conduct. His grade is holding at a C in reading. Mr. Jones insists Johnny can do better. Johnny prays for wisdom. He wished Jesus would speak out loud to him. Jesus could if He wanted to because He can do anything. Johnny believed it would be a lot easier if Jesus just told him what to do and what was going to happen. Johnny's mom

taught him that Jesus wants us to grow our faith. Though we can't see Jesus, He lives. Though we don't hear Him, He answers our prayers and guides us. Jesus is always at our right hand.

* * * * *

On the way home from school today, Johnny saw something near the bushes. It was small and brown in color. At first, he passed it by, but then Johnny went back and picked it up. Wow! A wallet. A wallet with $63. *Whoopee. Hooray. Finders keepers. I'm rich,* Johnny thought. *I can buy a skateboard right now. Should I tell my dad? No, I don't think so. He would tell me to take it to the police station or something. I really need a skateboard.*

After supper, Johnny took a shower and jumped in bed. He was so excited that he couldn't sleep. *Sixty-three dollars!* After a little while, Johnny began to feel badly. *If I have this wallet, then somebody doesn't have their wallet. They don't have their sixty-three dollars. They don't have their* plastic cards and pictures. *I think those must be grandkids' pictures because no-body can have that many kids.*

Johnny didn't pray and eventually fell asleep.

The next day at school, Johnny couldn't help but daydream about a brand-new skateboard. At times, he felt strange. Johnny took his seat in reading class.

BAM! Mrs. Carter said, "Put away your books and papers." She gave the class a quiz, a test.

Johnny didn't study last night. He was too excited and couldn't stop thinking about a shiny new skateboard. *I'm dead,* he thought. Johnny failed the quiz.

Johnny was troubled as he walked home from school. After supper, he went to his room and began his studies. "Dear Jesus, help me study. I need You." Johnny felt uneasy and prayed, "Dear Jesus, help me do the right thing with the wallet. I know it's not mine. I really do want that skateboard though. Amen."

Johnny grabbed the wallet and ran downstairs. "Dad! Dad!"

"What, Johnny?" he asked.

"Dad, I found this wallet. I really wanted to keep it. You know I want that skateboard. It has sixty-three dollars and junk in it. I think you should take it to the police station," Johnny replied.

His dad responded, "No, Son, I'm not going to take it to the police station."

Yeah! Now I get to keep it, Johnny thought.

"Son, you are going to take it to the police station and turn it in. I am so proud of you for doing the right thing."

Johnny really didn't want to turn it in; he just felt he had to. *Jesus would want me to return the wallet,* he thought.

* * * * *

The next morning Johnny and his dad arrived at the police station. Johnny carried the wallet inside and handed it to a policeman. The officer said, "Thank you, please wait here a minute."

Johnny and his dad took a seat in the foyer. The tallest man Johnny had ever seen came out and shook his and his dad's hand. He had to be over nine feet tall, like Goliath in the Bible.

The officer introduced himself and explained, "The man who lost this wallet reported it missing two days ago. He also left a generous reward to whoever turned it in. That would be you, Mr. Jones."

Mr. Jones said, "Oh no, that would be to Johnny, my son. He found it and he is turning it in."

The officer continued, "Mr. Boudreaux is ecstatic. All of his credit cards, his driver's license, and his grandchildren's pictures will be returned. Mr. Jones, you must be proud of Little Johnny here. Many kids wouldn't do the right thing in this day and age. There's still hope in the world."

Johnny received a $200 reward. Saturday morning, Mr. Jones was delighted to take Johnny to the store and allow him to pick out a skateboard. *Thank You, Jesus, for my new skateboard and for the man getting his wallet back. Amen,* Johnny prayed silently. The remainder of the reward money went in Johnny's college account.

"You shall not steal."

Exodus 20:15 NASB

30.

Johnny and Paul's Fishing Disaster

Mr. Burns, Johnny and Paul fished all summer. Johnny learned many fishing tips from Mr. Burns. He learned to fish where seagulls were diving in the water to eat baitfish. The bait was usually shad, but sometimes it was shrimp. Once, Mr. Burns and Johnny came upon working seagulls. Johnny could see the shrimp slapping the top of the water. It sounded like it was raining. It was really something to see. During the frenzy, you could throw just about anything on a hook and catch a fish. Once, they were out of bait. Mr. Burns said, "Use this and throw it." It was a wad of a white plastic bag. Johnny thought that was crazy, but he did as he

was told and caught 14 big speckled trout. How awesome is that?

After school today, Johnny visited Mr. Burns and asked if they were going fishing tomorrow. Mr. Burns apologized and said he wished he could, but he had to get his truck repaired. Johnny was certainly disappointed; he had his heart set on going fishing. Johnny understood and hoped to go fishing again soon. He asked, "Coming to church with us again this Sunday?"

Mr. Burns replied, "Wouldn't miss it for anything."

Johnny moped all the way home. Then it dawned on him. He and Paul could go fishing. They didn't have to wait for Mr.

Burns. Johnny has a tiny boat, and he could drag it to the shore. It wasn't that far if the boys cut through the empty fields nearby. Johnny can throw the cast net for bait, and he even had frozen shrimp in the freezer. *Yeah, that's it, I've got to call Paul*, he thought.

Johnny called Paul. Paul was excited. They both made sure it was okay with their parents. Johnny's dad said, "Just be sure to stay close to shore, Son." Johnny assured him they would. The boys got busy gathering snacks, finding fishing clothes, and hunting for their own rod and reel.

Paul spent the night at Johnny's house. They got up early the next morning. The boys placed their cooler in the boat and began dragging it to the bay. It was still dark and nice to hear the hear hoot owls and croaking frogs. Lightning bugs lit up their path to the bay. Paul didn't know what a lightning bug was, so they stopped and caught a few. Johnny mashed one on Paul's shirt. At first, Paul thought that was gross, but then he liked the way his shirt glowed in shimmering glitter. They went back to dragging the boat and made it to the beach. The water was smooth. Both hoped the fish would be hungry.

Almost immediately, Johnny got a nibble. There wasn't any current, so they didn't pitch an anchor. Paul caught the first trout. Johnny began catching a few as well. Eventually, they ran out of bait, so Johnny threw the cast net. He caught shad and shrimp. That's never happened before. Their boat did drift a bit, but not enough to worry about. They were telling stories and keeping up with the fish count. Things couldn't have been better.

Midmorning, Johnny and Paul ate their snack. Afterward, Johnny was the first to rebait. As he went to cast, he realized he couldn't see land. No land anywhere in sight! They had no idea they had been drifting. Johnny and Paul were miles from shore. They were lost!

Johnny thought, *I'm the captain. I've got to keep Paul safe.* Terrified, Johnny prayed out loud, "Dear Jesus. Please help us get home. Give me wisdom."

Paul said, "Amen!"

Johnny looked up to heaven and said, "Your Word tells me not to be afraid. You are in control. You made the whole universe. You parted the waters for Moses. You are the Miracle Maker. Give me wisdom. Please help us get home." Johnny reassured Paul they would get home.

Johnny remembered the sun rises in the east. The opposite way was west. "We need to go west. Let's paddle this way," Johnny said. They paddled hard, but the current was picking up. The boys were quickly heading farther out to sea.

Johnny could see a marker buoy just ahead. "Paul, we have to get to that buoy. Paddle hard!" The buoy was quickly approaching. The water current was pushing the boat at top speed!

Johnny was in the front of the boat. He grabbed the buoy and jumped out of the boat.

Paul was too far out. Paul screamed, "I can't reach it. I CAN'T swim!"

I've got to save Paul! Johnny reached out with all his might and grabbed Paul's shirt. Johnny yanked Paul out of the boat and threw him onto the buoy. The empty boat was now racing out to sea, and seconds later, Johnny couldn't see it anymore. Johnny said quietly, *Thank You, Jesus, for helping us to safety.*

* * * * *

For two days and two nights, they were stranded on that buoy. It was hot during the day, and cool during the night. They saw fish go by, even sharks chasing smaller fish. They weren't scared of the sharks though; they thought they were cool. Johnny and Paul were hungry and thirsty. They knew the danger in drinking the saltwater that surrounded them.

Paul had a can of tobacco in his pocket. Johnny asked him, "What are you doing with that? Are you crazy? Don't you know that stuff can kill you? It's not good, man."

Paul answered, "Well yeah, but I didn't know what it was. As it floated by, I just scooped it up. You were asleep."

"Give it to me," Johnny demanded. Johnny dumped out the watery tobacco and just kept the lid. It was shiny. "I'm going to try to flash at those boats. Let's pray."

Paul was all for praying.

Johnny prayed, "Dear Jesus, please let those people see us here and save us now." They were so keyed up they didn't even say amen.

Johnny went to jumping and waving and flashing the tin and praying out loud, "*You* can do all things. *You* desire to give me a hope and a future. *You* tell me to be still and know that *You* are God. From where does my help come? It comes from *You* and I need *Your* help right now."

At that moment, one of the boats in the far distance, began blowing his horn. It was loud. Paul screamed, "Oh man, thank You, Jesus!"

* * * * *

Things were awful back home. Their families and classmates were worried and afraid Johnny and Paul had died.

A prayer chain went out for Johnny and Paul on Saturday when they didn't come home. The local news station came out and did a story. It was on the news that evening. Paul's parents were especially depressed and despondent. Johnny's parents were better because they had faith and **knew** they would see Johnny soon. Mr. Burns stayed close.

The captain of the rescue boat called the U.S. Coast Guard and informed them he found the two lost boys on a buoy at the mouth of the Mississippi River. He asked for an ambulance to be at the dock upon their arrival. The U.S. Coast Guard did better; they had a medical helicopter land at the marina.

Johnny and Paul had a little trouble climbing into the strangers' boat. Once onboard, they fell limp; they had no energy. Paul's lips were cracked and bleeding. Johnny's lips weren't as bad. Both were sunburned, but not severely. As hungry as they had been, they weren't hungry now. The captain gave them Gatorade and insisted they drink it. They did.

Both sets of parents were waiting on the dock. News cameramen were on site filming everything for the five o'clock newscast. Mr. Burns looked like he was going to cry. The captain transporting Johnny and Paul, idled up to the dock. The boys were so weak, they had to be carried off the boat. Everyone felt better when they gave a thumbs up sign and smiled. Paramedics loaded Johnny and Paul into the helicopter and they were flown to the nearest hospital.

Mr. Jones led prayer in the emergency room. He praised and thanked God for the kids' safe return home. Paul's parents joined in. They had never prayed together before. Mr. Burns invited Paul's parents to church next Sunday, but told them they would have to drive themselves. He explained he rides with the Joneses, and their car is already packed full.

Everyone laughed.

* * * * *

Days later, Johnny and Paul were being discharged from the hospital. Their family and classmates were waiting outside the hospital doors. Many were holding up signs of "We LOVE You" and "Welcome Back."

Several TV reporters were present and filming. One reporter stuck his microphone at Johnny's mouth and asked, "What do you have to say, Johnny?"

Johnny answered, "Well, first I have to say God is so good, and I didn't know I knew that many scriptures. I want to learn more."

Then the reporter asked Paul what he had to say.

Paul responded, "I think next time we go fishing, we are going to go with our good friend Captain Burns."

Mr. Burns teared up.

> *"Call upon Me in the day of trouble; I shall rescue you, and you will honor Me."*
>
> Psalm 50:15 NASB

31.

Tip's in a Fight

Tip Tilman was a young boy born with severe weakness in his legs. He could walk a short distance as long as he had something to hold on to. Tip was confined to his wheelchair. But with hard work, he managed to do many of the things other kids could do.

Tip loved going hunting and fishing. In the boat, Tip would strap himself into the chair next to his dad. He got excited when a fish would hit his line and almost pull his fishing rod out of his hands. His dad enjoyed listening to him when that happened.

"Yeah, I've got you now, big boy. Sha-bam-a-llama!" yelled Tip. He couldn't wait to see what the fish was when he reeled it in close to the boat. Mr. Tilman would grab the net and scoop it up. "Yeah, baby!" Tip would holler as he high-fived his dad.

When they went hunting, Tip wheeled himself down the dirt road as close to his stand as possible. Then he would grab his dad's neck and ride him piggyback to his deer stand. It was so much fun. Tip always wanted to laugh, but he didn't. He didn't want to scare off any deer nearby.

After helping Tip into his hunting stand, Mr. Tilman went back and camouflaged the wheelchair. He hiked farther down the road and sat on a tree stump. Mr. Tilman thought of the day Tip shot his first deer. The way Tip told the story, you would have thought it was a huge twelve point or something. In reality, it was just a spike buck.

The company Mr. Tilman works for requires him to transfer out of state on occasion. The family moves once every two to three years. Most students at Tip's new schools were nice. Tip has no trouble making friends because he's such a likeable guy. In two days, Tip will start attending another new school. Being the "new kid" in school makes him a bit nervous, but he's used to it.

Tip settles into his classes. It's a challenge trying to learn so many names in just one day. He likes all his teachers, and they seem to genuinely like him. Tip likes going to school.

It takes Tip longer than most to go to the bathroom because of his disability. Today, Tip left his wheelchair outside the stall as he held onto the rail and went in.

Mike walked into the bathroom with two of his buddies. All of the kids call him "Big Mike," and he's mean. When he saw the wheelchair, he asked, "Hey, is this your wheelchair out here?"

Tip answered, "Yeah, I'm Tip. Be out in a few."

Mike responded, "Take your time, Bro." Big Mike pushed Tip's wheelchair out into the hallway. When Tip tried to open the stall door, Mike held it shut and wouldn't let him out.

Now, that's not nice, Tip thought. He asked, "Come on, man. Please let me out." Tip was embarrassed. He could hear Mike and his buddies snicker.

At that very moment, Johnny walked in. He realized what was going on. Johnny wanted to be a godly kid and often prayed that God would use him in a mighty way like he did King David. He believed all that God did for David, Gideon and Solomon, He could certainly do for him, too.

Johnny yells, "Stop that right now! Let him out!"

Big Mike laughed.

That was really the wrong thing to do. In a flash, Johnny grabbed Mike and threw him toward the bathroom door. Mike hit the door hard and fell to the ground. He almost cried. Mike's buddies helped him up and the three ran away.

Tip hobbled out of the bathroom stall.

Johnny brought his wheelchair to him. "Hi, I'm Johnny. I'm your new best friend, man. You new here?"

Tip answered, "Sure am. We just moved here. My dad works at the chemical plant. We move a lot. I'm Tip."

"Great. Want to go to the movies Saturday night?" Johnny asked.

"Sounds good, man," Tip replied. *This guy is different from most. I like him.* He was glad Johnny didn't make fun of him or say anything about what had just happened.

* * * * *

At 3:30 the school let out. All the students are preparing to go home. Tip will be riding the same bus as Johnny and Mean Mike and his buddies. Tip wheeled himself onto the bus first and sat next to the bus driver. Mean Mike and his buddies got on the bus next. They talked smack to Tip and took their seats. Last of all, Johnny got on the bus, and you guessed it—the bad boys shut their traps. They were afraid to say anything ugly with Johnny around.

Mike and his buddies got off the bus two stops ahead of Tip. Then Tip got off and Johnny got off after the next stop. Johnny ran as fast as he could back to Tip's house. He was afraid there might be trouble.

Sure enough, as Tip made it to his front door, one of Mike's buddies grabbed Tip's wheelchair. Big Mike pushed Tip, causing him to fall to the ground. Tip was furious. Mike started laughing. One of the kids kicked the wheelchair away. Out of nowhere, Johnny appeared. He knocked one kid to the ground so fast, the kid didn't know what hit him. Tip rolled over on top of him and started smacking him good. Johnny threw one punch and knocked the other boy out cold. He was laying limp on the ground. Johnny zeroed in on Big Mike.

Unbelievable! Big Mike's running away! Johnny chased him and tackled him to the ground. Dirt and grass were being thrown into the air as they tussled. Johnny could have really beat him up, but he didn't. He jerked Mike up and grabbed both of his shoulders very tightly.

Mike couldn't get away. He told Mike that Tip better not have any more trouble from him **ever** again. "Understand, man?" Johnny insisted.

Mike nodded yes.

Johnny hurried to pull Tip off the other guy. Tip was still knocking him around. Tip had never been in a fight before. He was really mad and couldn't stop himself. Tip was surprised how badly that kid looked. He felt guilty for taking all of his anger on this poor kid. Both of Mike's buddies hobbled off and met up with Mike.

Tip's mom drove up. When she got out of the car and saw Tip, she became hysterical and started to cry. "What happened? Are you okay?"

Johnny was helping Tip back into his wheelchair. Tip was constantly telling his mom he was okay and to relax. She ran into the house and got an ice pack and ran back. She handed it to Tip, and he placed it over his red and swollen eye. He said, "By the way, Mom, this is my friend Johnny. Can I go to the movie with him tomorrow?"

"Sure, Tip, you can go. Nice to meet you, Johnny. Thank you for being kind and helping Tip out," she said.

Johnny headed home. Tip was glad his mom met Johnny. They went inside. Tip started doing his homework, and Mrs. Tilman calmed down. When Tip heard his dad drive up, he put his wheelchair in gear and flew out the front door.

"Dad, Dad, you won't believe what happened. I was in a fight. It was great. Can you believe it?" Tip yelled.

Mr. Tilman was confused. *Tip in a fight? It was great? I don't think so.* He followed Tip into the house. He asked Tip to slow down and tell him exactly what had happened.

Tip told his dad what happened from start to finish, and he didn't skip a detail.

Mr. Tilman asked how the other kid was.

Tip smiled proudly. "He's bad, Dad. Real bad! I gave him a good lickin'."

Mr. Tilman wasn't smiling. "Just because you can, doesn't mean you should. Only hit once or twice if you can. Just enough to put an end to the trouble. Do you understand? Remember, try to think about what Jesus would want you to do."

Tip thought he would be proud of him for taking up for himself and actually winning the battle. "Okay, Dad, I understand. I did feel bad when I saw his bloody nose and lips."

Mr. Tilman continued, "Tip, you felt convicted. That was Jesus letting you know you went too far. Pray about it, and please, don't ever brag about fighting. That's really nothing to feel proud about."

Tip answered, "Sure, Dad. Me and Jesus will have a talk and straighten everything out. I want you to meet Johnny tomorrow. He's a great kid. I think we'll be friends forever."

One who has unreliable friends soon comes to ruin, but there is a friend who sticks closer than a brother.

Proverbs 18:24 NIV

32.

Johnny in Jail?

Johnny's doing well in school. He's still a bit of a prankster and likes to have fun. Yesterday, Trey dared him to put a snake in their teacher's desk.

Johnny was so sneaky. Today, he walked into the classroom and up to Mrs. Walker's desk. Johnny sat on the edge of her desk as the other students were coming into the room. He pretended to study the blackboard, and he slipped his hand that held the snake down to the desk drawer. He opened the drawer slightly, then let the snake go. He gently closed the drawer quickly so the snake wouldn't get out. The grass snake was completely harmless.

All the children took their seats. Johnny couldn't wait to see Mrs. Walker open the drawer. The kids sat with excitement. Here she comes.

Mrs. Walker sat at her desk and prepared to take roll call. She opened her desk drawer to grab a pen. The snake bolts out, and Mrs. Walker squeals at the top of her lungs. She races to the door and screams, "Children out, now!"

The kids got up quickly and filed out of their classroom. Johnny burst out in laughter. It was just too funny. "Mrs. Walker, it's just a grass snake. It can't harm you. I'll get it," he said.

Mrs. Walker was almost crying, but the kids were all laughing. Johnny then chased the snake down and caught it. All the while, Mrs. Walker is telling him to leave it alone. Johnny dropped the snake out the window.

As the children went back to take their seats, Mrs. Walker called Johnny to her desk. "Johnny Jones, did you put that snake in my desk?" she demanded.

"Yes, but it can't hurt anyone," he replied.

Mrs. Walker sent Johnny to Mr. Cameron, the principal. What was Johnny thinking? Mrs. Walker didn't open another desk drawer all day.

* * * * *

Mrs. Walker is Johnny's mom's friend. Mr. Cameron attends Johnny's church, and his secretary teaches Sunday school there. They were all somewhat miffed at Johnny's behavior. Mr. Cameron called Johnny's dad and placed him on speaker. "Mr. Jones, Johnny's prank with the snake today in Mrs. Walker's class is totally unacceptable. The children and Mrs. Walker could have been seriously hurt in a panic. Johnny will have to serve two day's detention."

Mr. Jones understood and said, "Johnny, I will talk to you when I get home."

That evening, Mr. Jones and Johnny had a discussion on acceptable behavior in school. Johnny already knew scaring anyone with a snake was wrong. He just can't resist a dare. Mr. Jones asked, "Johnny, if all the kids told you to jump off a cliff, would you do it?" Johnny nodded no. He continued, "When are you going to start making good decisions? Trey and all the kids are still laughing. How about you? You still think this is funny?" Johnny nodded no.

All Johnny could think about was facing everyone at church on Sunday. He was ashamed.

Church service was fine. Everybody was nice and all was forgiven. Johnny learned his lesson — no more pranks.

* * * * *

A few years went by, Johnny's parents were very proud of him. Mr. Jones trusted Johnny and allowed him to drive the family car. Johnny was even allowed to take his buddies with him sometimes. None of the other parents would allow that.

Johnny picked up Blake, Hayden and Shane to go to a party. Blake wanted to stop and buy beer. Johnny stood firm. "Absolutely not!" Eventually, Blake talked Johnny into stopping so everyone could buy a soda.

Johnny stopped at the first gas station they came to. They all went in. Hayden and Shane grabbed drinks and chips. Blake went to the beer cooler. He secretly slipped a six-pack up under his jacket as the others were paying for their sodas. The four boys all walked out together and got into Johnny's car. They were off again.

About five minutes into the drive, Blake pulls out a beer and pops the top. He politely asked everyone if they wanted a beer. "Here, Johnny, take one."

Johnny flips out; he's enraged. "What did you do? Why would you do this? Are you crazy?"

Blake states, "C'mon, man, be cool. Sometimes you just have to cut loose." Then he put an opened beer right there in the console for Johnny.

The cashier at the store thought she saw one of the boys steal beer. Security cameras caught everything on film. Cops were called. They were on the lookout for Mr. Jones' car.

Out of the blue, Johnny heard sirens. Bright blue lights began flashing behind them. Blake threw his beer out his window. When the cop stopped and walked up to Johnny's window, he saw Johnny's beer. The officer ordered Johnny to step out of the car. Johnny was so shaken up, he couldn't think. Blake, Hayden and Shane got to call their parents and went home. The officer hand cuffed Johnny and hauled him to jail in the police car.

From jail, Johnny called his parents. All Johnny could say was, "I'm in jail. Please come get me out."

Mr. Jones was devastated and Mrs. Jones cried. When they arrived at the police station, they saw Johnny behind bars. Mrs. Jones cried even louder.

"Dad, it wasn't my beer. It really wasn't. Blake stole it. I didn't know he put one in the console. I'm in an awful mess." Johnny settled down and told them exactly what happened.

Johnny and his parents held hands and prayed God's will be done. They were at peace because this battle belonged to the Lord. It wasn't Johnny's. Mr. and Mrs. Jones had to leave and went home. Johnny stayed in jail overnight. He would see the judge in the morning.

Judge Jackson knows Johnny's entire family. Yep, they all go to the same church. After he was given all the details about Johnny's arrest, he had mercy on Johnny. The judge sentenced Johnny to six months of probation. He also had to serve two weeks of community service, talking to teenagers about the dangers of drinking and driving. It could have been much worse. Johnny was relieved!

Johnny prayed, "Dear Jesus, I thank You for taking *my* place on the cross to save me. Thank You for my parents who love and support me, and trust me. Thank You for seeing me through all of this. Thank You for Judge Jackson's decision. Please help me hang out with godly friends so I don't get into a mess like this ever again. And Jesus, I pray for Blake. Amen."

* * * * *

The righteous choose their friends carefully, but the way of the wicked leads them astray.

Proverbs 12:26 NIV

33.

Will Johnny Say NO to Drugs?

Johnny's parents taught him well. They rehearsed just about every scenario they could think of to prepare him for the world of drugs. They would say, "You know drugs hurt people. They can kill people. Don't do drugs son. Just say no and move on. You can't stop others, but you can stand strong for yourself. If you ever want to talk about anything, please come talk to us." Mr. and Mrs. Jones prayed for Johnny and Julie all the time.

Johnny told himself years ago he would never do drugs. No one would ever talk him into it. Our body is the temple of God. God literally lives within our heart. Johnny doesn't want to mess up God's house. The consequences for going against God's Word are serious, even dangerous.

Johnny remembered that when the Israelites were disobedient, they missed out on God's blessings. He wanted to live a life that pleased God. Johnny couldn't afford to miss out on any of his blessings.

* * * * *

Johnny and Wesley met at the public pool five or six summers ago. They swam there every week and quickly became friends. Each liked staying overnight at the other's house on occasion. They spent so much time together, people in town thought they were brothers.

On this particular night, Wesley rode with Johnny to the football game. After the game, the kids hung out at Ty's place. Everyone was drinking sodas, eating chips, and listening to music. Some kids were dancing, but most were just standing around talking. Two guys from another school arrived unannounced, Charles and Drake. They seemed polite and began mingling into the crowd. Late into the night, one of them opened up his jacket and there it was: powders, pills, vials and syringes. Most of the kids politely walked away. A few were curious and continued to talk to him. One of those kids was Wesley.

Wesley asked, "Do you take those pills?"

Charles answered, "Oh yeah, man. They are cool. You'll feel great. Nothing like it. Want to try something?"

Johnny butted in. "No, Charles, he doesn't want to try any. Let's go, Wesley!"

Wesley wouldn't leave. He didn't care what Johnny had to say.

Johnny wasn't sure what to do. Again, he demanded, "Let's leave, Wesley. We've got to go now."

Wesley refused.

Johnny went outside and called his dad. "Dad, there's a kid at the party offering everyone drugs. I can't get Wesley to leave!"

Johnny's dad said he would call the cops and head right over. He told Johnny to stay outside. But Johnny was worried about Wesley, so he went back in to check on him. Johnny found Wesley sitting in a chair, slumped to the side, and sleeping.

Ty came up and said, "Johnny, he took some pills. I told him not to. I tried to stop him, but you know Wesley. He likes to be noticed. I'm sorry. I hope he's okay."

Johnny tried to wake Wesley, but couldn't. He called 911. The cops showed up, Johnny's dad showed up, and an ambulance arrived. All the kids, except for Johnny and Ty, went home.

Johnny stayed near Wesley and began praying for him. The paramedics ran to Wesley's side, took his pulse, and checked for breathing. They rushed him to the hospital.

Johnny rode with his dad to the hospital. Johnny was crying and explaining how he told Wesley not to do anything stupid and to leave. Mr. Jones was very worried about Wesley, but he was also thankful Johnny made the right decision not to take drugs. At the hospital, Johnny's dad encouraged everyone to grab hands and prayed for Wesley's full recovery.

The doctor came out to the waiting room and said, "I'm sorry. We did all we could do, but it was too late. He's gone." Wesley's mom broke down. Everyone started to cry.

Johnny felt guilty. He should have made Wesley leave. He wished he would have knocked him out and dragged him home.

* * * * *

Two days later, the phone rang. It was Wesley's mom. She asked Johnny to speak at Wesley's funeral. Johnny agreed, but he really didn't want to.

The church was jam-packed. Beautiful flowers were everywhere. All the seats were taken, and people were standing anywhere they could find a spot. Many were forced to stand outside the church. Everyone was mourning Wesley's passing.

One little boy asked his grandmother, "Mommies and daddies shouldn't have to bury their kids, should they, Grandma?"

She answered, "No, they really shouldn't."

It was an emotional ceremony for all. Pictures of Wesley, with his contagious smile, flashed on the screen behind the pulpit. You couldn't help but smile when you saw his face. Wesley's mom was inconsolable at first, but she's quiet now. Johnny is about to speak. You could have heard a pin drop.

"Wesley was my best friend. He was a really good kid and hardly ever did anything bad. I am going to miss him a lot. Wesley is in the arms of Jesus. Jesus, who is here and with each us right now. Wesley accepted Jesus as his Savior a few years ago, here in this very church. Jesus has a home in heaven for those of us who have accepted him as Lord and

Savior. I'm sad he's gone, but when I think of Wesley with Jesus, it makes me happy. I will see him again, and so will you.

"The devil makes terrible things seem good. That's why he's the master deceiver, a liar. Wesley made *one* horrible decision, just *one*. He tried drugs, once. It was that *one* act, *one* terrible choice, that cost Wesley his life. Wesley's mom wants you to say no to drugs."

"The thief comes only to steal and kill and destroy; I have come that they may have life, and have it to the full."

John 10:10 NASB

Put on the full armor of God, so that you will be able to stand firm against the schemes of the devil.

Ephesians 6:11 NASB

34.

Oh No, Eric Goes to Prison!

Years ago, the Towns family moved in near Johnny. At the time, they had an eight-year-old boy named Eric and six-year-old daughter named Bella. Johnny's family introduced themselves to Mr. and Mrs. Towns, and soon they became friends. Some weekends they barbequed together. Eric and Johnny liked to challenge Bella and Julie in competing games. It was fun for sure.

Johnny watched Eric pull his sister's hair "accidentally." Sometimes he would trip her "accidentally." Eric thought it was funny, but it wasn't. Bella didn't like it.

Johnny got a car on his sixteenth birthday. A month later, Eric got a truck on his birthday. Johnny and Eric's parents taught them to drive slowly, watch for kids in the street, and stay off their cell phone while driving. Eric's dad tried to impress upon him the seriousness of driving a vehicle and how horrible it would be to have an accident and hurt himself or someone else.

Eric heard that many times, but he could have cared less.

After a year of driving with a parent at their side, Eric and Johnny can legally drive a car all by themselves. They felt free. They believed they were grown. Eric loved running errands for his mom. He drove safely if anyone was around, but if he didn't think anyone was looking, he drove recklessly. Eric's parents would have thrown a fit if they knew that.

Not long after, Johnny and his buddies asked Eric for a ride after school. Eric was happy to oblige. When the boys got in his truck, Eric drove like a maniac. He started doing donuts in the parking lot and then spun out, burning rubber and leaving smoke behind. The boys tried not to show it, but they were scared. That was it. Johnny had to tell his dad about Eric's driving.

That evening, Johnny told his dad the whole story. Mr. Jones went straight over to Eric's house. Eric was at the library and wasn't home just yet. Mr. Jones explained everything to Eric's dad.

"Not my Eric. He would never!" replied Mr. Towns. He got angry and told Mr. Jones to leave his house.

Johnny's dad politely left and went home. After that, the neighbors weren't friends anymore. How sad.

* * * * *

Eric graduated from high school and started college, but later quit. He said he was going to get a job, but didn't. Eric preferred to stay home and watch television. He stayed up late at night and slept all day.

One night, Eric went out for pizza. He was driving 87 mph when his cell phone rang. Eric was wiggling around trying to retrieve his phone from his back pocket. BAM! He crashed! His truck spun around, went off the highway, and then back onto the highway. You could hear cars slamming into one another, screeching sounds and honking horns. Eric's air bag deployed, and he was dazed when he came to a stop. He could smell oil and burning rubber.

Soon the fire department and multiple cop cars and ambulances arrived. Pieces of cars were strewn about the highway. Two vehicles were smoking and one was on fire. Eric was able to get out of his truck. He wasn't hurt and called his dad.

Firefighters had to cut one car open to get a man, woman and child out. The woman and child were taken by helicopter to the nearest hospital. The man was taken by ambulance to the hospital. The woman and a four-year-old girl went straight to emergency surgery. The man received stitches and a cast for a broken arm.

When Mr. Towns got to the scene, Eric kept saying over and over, "Dad, it's not my fault. I didn't do anything wrong. It was an accident. That's why they call it an accident."

Eric's dad was furious. He had heard that two people were air lifted to the emergency room. It had to be serious. "Hush. Not another word, Son," he snapped. "Do you realize people are hurt—some may not make it?"

Eric didn't care. He only cared about himself. Just then, a police officer approached Eric and explained that Eric had caused the accident. Eric rammed the vehicle in front of him, which caused a chain reaction and multiple car pileup. Firemen were still checking vehicles to see if others were injured and in need medical attention.

At that moment, Mr. Towns remembered what Johnny's dad told him—that Eric was reported as driving carelessly. Oh my, Eric was doing wrong!

Eric's dad dropped to his knees. "Dear God, forgive me for all my shortcomings. Help me be a better father to Eric. But most of all, please help those poor people in the emergency room. I pray none of them die. Take their pain away and make Your presence known to them. Amen."

Eric heard his dad pray out loud, but he didn't pray.

Johnny and his dad happened to drive by the scene. When they saw Mr. Towns, they stopped and got out of their car.

All Eric's dad could say was, "I'm sorry. I'm so sorry. What's wrong with me? Why did I get mad at you and tell you to leave my house? You were only trying to help me. I did nothing. Now look at what's happened. Those poor people."

Johnny's dad was kind and asked if he could drive Mr. Towns and Eric to the hospital.

"Oh yes, absolutely," Mr. Towns replied. "I must know if they are going to be all right."

At the hospital, Mr. Jones led a prayer for everyone involved in the accident, especially the woman and child in emergency surgery. The doctors came out and announced that after a long recovery, everyone would be okay. Mr. Jones and Mr. Towns were relieved.

Eventually, Eric went on trial for driving recklessly and causing serious injury. The poor little girl had to go through a year of rehabilitation. It was hard and painful for her. Mr. Towns ached for her. Eric had never said he was sorry, but his dad sure did.

Before the judge sentenced Eric (that's giving him his punishment), Eric spoke. "It was an accident. It wasn't my fault. I'm the victim here. You've got to let me go," he pleaded.

The judge was furious and sentenced him to twenty-five years in prison.

Eric started crying uncontrollably.

His dad cried too, mostly because his son wasn't sorry for what he had done.

Eric screamed, "Dad, help me! You know it wasn't my fault. I don't want to go to jail! Get me out!"

To prison he went. Eric was in jail with some seriously bad guys. He was scared. Eric had to learn to get along with people. Day in and day out, Eric did the same thing over and over. At night, he would lay in bed and think. He had a lot of time to think.

Folsom Prison offered educational and Bible study classes. Eric took a Bible course. The more he learned, the more awesome the Bible became to him. Eric took every Bible class available. He learned that God loves him unconditionally, no matter what. He learned that King David had a man murdered and thought he could hide it from God. Nothing is hidden from God. Famous people in the Bible did terrible things, but after asking God to forgive them, God forgave them, restored them, and even blessed them.

Eric gave his heart to Jesus and was saved. He became a new man. The old Eric was gone forever. He began thinking of others and praying for them. Eric encouraged other inmates to take Bible classes. He told everyone Jesus loved them. Eric explained their Father in heaven desires that they all be saved and not perish. Some listened, some didn't. Many were glad Eric was learning the Bible, others thought he was nuts. Eric only cared about what God thought.

Eric took the commandment to go and tell others about Jesus seriously. He longed to please his Savior, Christ Jesus. Eric couldn't wait for his parents to visit so he could tell them the good news.

* * * * *

Johnny rode with Mr. and Mrs. Towns to visit Eric in prison today.

Eric was glad to see them all and blurted out, "I'm saved. I'm going to heaven just like y'all. Jesus is so good!" He kept talking about Jesus and what Jesus had done for him. "God created each of us for a reason, and I hope to do whatever it is God wants from me." Eric was thankful he was allowed to listen to gospel music every day. He told his dad, "Sometimes I catch myself boogying. I'm so happy." Eric couldn't stop smiling. He truly was a "new" man. His parents will tell you that this man is not the same man who caused the terrible accident that night long ago. They were thrilled. Eric continued his studies. He has faith God will direct his path when he gets released from prison.

Johnny was glad to see the change in his friend!

Jesus replied: "'Love the Lord your God with all your heart and with all your soul and with all your mind.' This is the first and greatest commandment. And the second is like it: 'Love your neighbor as yourself.'"

Matthew 22:37–39 NIV

No one should seek their own good, but the good of others.

1 Corinthians 10:24 NIV

35.

Big-Eared Brad Benton

One evening, Johnny was sitting out on the swing with Mr. Burns, watching their dogs, Jack and Trigger, play chase together. They talk a lot on that swing. I think they are best of friends. On this particular day, Mr. Burns told Johnny the story about a man named Brad Benton.

Brand Benton is a smart, kind, hard-working man. He always has been. He was brought up by parents who really encouraged him to do his very best all the time, no matter what.

Poor Brad had it bad as a kid, though. You see, he had big ears. I'm not talking just big ears; I mean, huge ears. Ugly ears to everyone except his family. When Brad's mom took him into the grocery store, people would stare at Brad's ears. Very small kids would innocently ask, "Why does that boy have big ears, Mommy?" Older children would laugh at him. It was awkward.

For a long time, Brad was troubled by the size of his ears. But as Brad got older and learned about God, he actually liked his ears. God doesn't make mistakes. Brad had big ears because he was supposed to have big ears. If someone didn't like his ears, that was their problem, not his.

In school, Brad made the best grades. He played sports well, too. He gave it all he had, just as he was taught. Students from rival schools were especially cruel. Brad didn't mind; his teammates looked up to him. Brad had great character. Plus, Brad scored more points in a basketball game than the rest of the team combined. Brad made the whole team look good. They won most games.

Eventually, Brad went to college and graduated with an engineering degree in three years, not four like most students. He applied for jobs immediately. Brad wanted to earn his own money. Brad Benton landed the best job ever! Joe's Engineering International hired him and paid him very well. Brad went to work 15 minutes early every day and was always the last employee to leave for the day. He loved his job and wanted the company to succeed.

Many of the workers wouldn't talk to Brad. Some would chuckle and leave the room when he entered. Even Brad's supervisor gave him a hard time. Brad was the model employee and brushed it off. When his co-workers didn't do their job, Brad did it. He figured he was there to work, so he worked. One man took notice, the owner, Mr. Glass.

Mr. Glass was a tough, no-nonsense kind of guy. Many years ago, he was hanging out with a few construction workers playing pool. A thief stole Joe's coat when his back was turned. Joe saw it hanging on another man's chair and re-spectfully asked for it back. The idiot had the nerve to tell Joe that the coat wasn't his and refused to give it back. WHAM! One punch right to the kisser, and the poor fellow hit the floor with a twisted nose and bloody mouth. Two of the thief's teeth were now laying on his chin! Joe took his coat back. Word got around quickly, "Don't mess with Joe!"

Many years have since passed. Mr. Glass is elderly. He has no children or grandchildren. He alone owned Joe's Engineering International. He was trying to decide how best to take care of his employees when he retired. Then it came to him: Brad Benton.

Mr. Glass watched Brad day in and day out. He was impressed with Brad's work ethic. Brad saw to it things were done correctly. Mr. Glass admired the way Brad handled himself. *Who else would care about my company like Brad does? No one. That's it. Boy, is Brad going to be shocked when I call him to a meeting tomorrow. I'm going to give him my company.*

The next morning, Brad went to work early as usual. Mr. Glass came in early this morning, too, and went straight to his office. Brad was surprised by that. Mr. Glass called a company-wide meeting in the break area for 10:00 a.m. He had his secretary set out pastries and drinks.

Just before 10:00 a.m., employees met in the break area. They were serving themselves and wondering what all the fuss was about. Some were afraid of a layoff. Others thought the company was being bought out by a competitor. Most didn't care; they were enjoying donuts! Brad worked right up until 9:59, and then he walked into the break area exactly at 10:00 a.m.

Mr. Glass walked out of his office and into the break room. He was smiling so big. He was thinking, *What is Brad going to think about this? What is he going to do? This is going to be so much fun.*

"Glad all of you are here. Hope you're enjoying the donuts and coffee. I have made a rather important decision. You see, I'm retiring. I have no children or grandchildren. I want you all to be well taken care of when I leave.

"That's what I've tried to do for you—give you a great job with great benefits. That only happens when the owner loves the job and his employees. So, while I was determining what to do with my company, that was what I was thinking: 'God, who loves the job, this company, and the employees like I do?' And boy, did God answer. Many of you might regret some of the things you've done or said here at Joe's Engineering."

Some of the supervisors thought surely Mr. Glass would pick them to take over the company, because they had worked for Joe's Engineering many years. Imagine their surprise when Mr. Glass said, "Mr. Brad Benton, COME ON DOWN. YOU ARE THE NEW OWNER OF JOE'S ENGINEERING INTERNATIONAL!"

Big-Eared Brad Benton got all choked up. He thought, *There must be another Brad Benton. He can't be talking about me.* Nope, Mr. Glass was definitely talking about this Brad Benton. Brad started walking toward Mr. Glass. He was totally surprised by the announcement and had no idea Mr. Glass even knew who he was.

Mr. Glass stuck out his hand and shook Brad's hand. "Son, I think you will do a fine job. I want you to have the company. I'm giving it to you. Do you accept the job?"

Brad answered, "As God is my witness, I surely do. And I will talk to Him every day about having the wisdom of Solomon to care for and lead all these people."

Mr. Glass replied, "Great. It's a done deal."

* * * * *

Mr. Burns chuckled and continued:

"The next morning, Brad went to his new office wearing his regular uniform. He checked in, checked the computer, checked his calendar, and then walked out to the shop and all over the plant. Now, the people that used to ignore Brad or say something ugly to him, were now saying, 'Good morning, Mr. Benton. How are you this morning, sir?' They all were actually doing their job because they no longer had Brad to dump it on.

"Isn't that something? It doesn't get much better than that, does it, Johnny?

"You see, they didn't care about Brad or even take notice of all the good he did, but God sure did. Our God doesn't miss a thing. He sees it all. And the most important thing is, He KNOWS our hearts. He knows when we are trying to trick someone, or when we are just showing off. God chose to bless Brad in a huge way, didn't he?"

Johnny answered, "He sure did, Mr. Burns. I've got to tell Memaw this story. She's going to love it. She's always telling us stories. She really likes stories about how good our God is. She likes to brag on Him. Like the Bible says, 'Let him who boasts, boast in the Lord.' That means, if we brag, we brag on the Lord, not on ourselves or anyone else."

The eyes of the LORD are in every place, watching the evil and the good.

Proverbs 15:3 NASB

36.

Jehovah-Jireh (The Lord Will Provide)

Sally has just arrived in New Orleans with her three children: two boys and a girl. The oldest child is Billy, but everyone calls him Bubba. Bubba is six, and his brother, Beckham, is four. The two-year-old little girl has the sweetest eyes and long curly golden-brown hair. The boys take good care of her and call her Tink.

Bubba helps his mom unload the truck and haul the items into their new house. Sally was broke. She spent all her money on the move to New Orleans. The radio in the car didn't work. The TV isn't hooked up. Sally's cell phone is dead and needs recharging. Everyone is tired. Sally opened a large can of ravioli and heated it in the microwave.

As Bubba helped Tink eat, his mom reassembled her bed. She hunted through the boxes and found sheets and blankets. After tucking in the sheets, Sally covered the king-sized bed with a large blanket. After the kids ate, each took a bath and went to bed. Exhausted, they dozed off quickly. Sally went to bed thinking about the many needs of tomorrow and fell asleep.

About two o'clock in the morning, Sally got up to go to the bathroom. As her feet hit the floor, they made a big splash in cold dirty water. Sally's standing in nearly two feet of water. The house is flooded. She didn't know why. She tried to open the front door but couldn't. She looked outside and water was everywhere. Strong winds were blowing.

The water is rising quickly. She ran for a chair and dragged it to the attic entrance. She woke Bubba and lifted him into the attic first. She raced back and snatched up Tink and had Beckham climb onto her back and told him to hold on. It was hard for Sally to wade through the nasty water carrying two kids. Bubba grabbed Tink and helped her into the attic. Sally flipped Beckham around and practically threw him into the attic. Suddenly, Sally's legs were on fire. As soon as she got into the attic, she frantically squashed red ants that covered her legs. Sally made sure the children were okay and had no bug bites.

Sally never heard the Weather Channel reporting Hurricane Jane was heading up the mouth of the Mississippi River. People had been instructed to evacuate. The reports were to expect great devastation.

The water was still rising. It's up four feet. Spiders and bugs were floating on the water and beginning to crawl on the furniture and walls. Sally hoped they wouldn't come into the attic. She made the children as comfortable as possible, and they fell back asleep.

Sally prayed, "Please help me take care of my kids. Please keep them safe. Give me wisdom."

She got a glimpse outside through a vent. It was so dark out. She could barely make out trees. They were violently swirling and swaying. The wind started howling, and the house began to shake and make strange noises. Sally was frightened.

Praying should have been the first thing Sally did. Now, she couldn't stop praying! She knew God made the universe, and He holds it together by His hands. Sally remembered Joshua's prayer for the sun to stand still upon Gideon and the moon to stand still in the valley of Ayalon. God held the sun and moon in place for Joshua, in answer to his prayer. The only reason she could recall this was because of her grandpa.

Grandpa loved reading his Bible. It fascinated him. He loved telling Sally about the talking donkey and about Jonah being stuck inside a whale's stomach for three days.

Grandpa's favorite story was about Shadrach, Meshach and Abednego—the men thrown into a massive fire inside a furnace. The heat was so horrific, it killed the men standing outside the furnace. But God protected Shadrach, Meshach and Abednego while they walked around inside the fiery furnace. Flames of fire were up to their heads. The three men were laughing and shocked that they weren't being burned. They weren't hot. This was a miracle. God is the Miracle Maker.

Grandpa would laugh and say, "And then Jesus decided to show up and pay them a little visit right there in the middle of the flames. They didn't even smell like smoke when they came out." He would always say, "Our God truly is awesome!"

Sally meditated on that, on just how awesome God is. She prayed for her children, became calm, and fell asleep.

Something caused Sally to awaken. *Thank You, Lord, for keeping us safe,* she prayed as she looked down from the attic. The water was gone. Trash and sludge covered the floor. The smell was awful. Sally started to cry, but then she stopped herself. She didn't have time to cry; there was work to be done. Sally bailed out of the attic. All the packed boxes were now ruined. Sally did find a large ice chest outside. It was clean inside. She decided it would make a decent playpen for Tink.

A church bus parked in front of Sally's house. Twenty people came to the front door, or what was left of it. "Ma'am, we are here to help."

Sally told them thank you and asked what had happened.

"Hurricane Jane came in," they explained.

Wow, a hurricane! Really?

The mission team went straight to work. They ripped out sheet rock, pulled out carpet, swept out mud and trash. They had mops and Clorox and even toys for kids. Tink played in the ice chest. It was just her size.

One young man, Jake, walked right by Sally and casually said, "The Lord will provide."

Before noon, Tink and Beckham complained they were hungry. Sally was trying figure out what to do. All of her food was ruined.

Jake walked by again. "The Lord will provide."

Everyone heard a strange noise. It sounded like a dinner bell. The kids ran outside. It was the Red Cross. They had bowls of jambalaya. The nice man kept repeating, "Free lunches. Come one, come all. Free lunches. Come one, come all." Everyone got a bowl of jambalaya and ate. This was Sally and her children's first time to eat jambalaya. They loved it.

After a short break, the mission group went straight back to work and gutted the house. The sun was going down. Mosquitoes were beginning to come out. The windows were broken. Sally thought, *How am I going to keep my kids safe? We have no—*

"The Lord will provide," Jake said as he walked by.

A tractor pulling a trailer loaded with hay bales parked outside Sally's house.

The driver got off and walked in. "Ma'am, we would like to bring you and your children to the church tonight for safety. We have clean cots to sleep on, even clean clothing, if needed."

"Oh yes, thank you," she replied.

The kids ran to the tractor. Beckham hollered, "It's a hayride, Mom. Come on."

Jake walked right beside Sally and said, "The Lord will provide."

Riding on the hayride, Sally had to agree. God had provided everything they needed—absolutely everything.

At the church, everyone ate, bathed, and called it a night. The next morning, they all headed back to Sally's house to finish up.

Sheetrock had been delivered to Mr. Smith, Sally's next-door neighbor. A different mission team arrived at his house and began to install it.

After seeing the sheetrock next door, Sally prayed, "God, we need sheetrock. I need to get this house closed in so we can keep insects out. I have no money. I—"

Before she finished her prayer, Jake was coming in the front door carrying a piece of sheetrock. "The Lord will provide," he said.

Sally wondered how Jake could possibly know when she was praying and what she was asking for.

Mr. Smith was right behind Jake. "Ma'am, I'm John Smith. I live next door. I told the kids to bring my leftover sheetrock here and fix your house, if that's okay." Sally explained she could not pay for it. "Oh no, honey, I want you to have it. I ordered too much," he said.

"Thank you, sir, and it's very nice to meet you. I'm Sally Edmonds."

Sally went to her bedroom and dropped to her knees. "Thank You, God, for… Thank You, God for… Thank You, God for…" She named off all the blessings she could think of. Sally knew all that she had or ever will have, God supplied. God is in control. Nothing takes Him by surprise. She prayed for faith—faith like that Jake kid has.

Sally and her children rode the hayride back to the church for the night, but tomorrow night, they will be ready to stay at home.

Sally is determined never to be afraid again. She remembered that "do not be afraid" is written in the Bible 365 times. That's one "fear not" verse for every day of the year!

And my God will supply all your needs according to His riches in glory in Christ Jesus.

Philippians 4:19 NASB

37.

A Difference between Savior and Lord

Jean attended church with her family for years. She recognized that God had been speaking to her the last few Sundays. This Sunday was different; Jean got up, walked to the preacher, and accepted Jesus Christ as her Savior. She was fourteen and looked forward to being baptized completely underwater just like Jesus was.

Jean was well mannered. She continued to do well in school. She grew up, became a nurse, married Jim, and had a baby girl, Suzie. Jean tried to be the best wife, mother and nurse she could be. The family went to church regularly and enjoyed fellowship with like believers.

At age thirty-six, Jean had X-rays taken. The radiologist called her two days later with the results. Jean had a problem and needed surgery right away. That totally took her by surprise.

Surgery went well. After the incision healed, Jean followed up with monthly treatments that made her weak and nauseated. The only things that tasted good were pizza and Blue Bell ice cream. Just as she began regaining strength and feeling better, it was time to go in for her next treatment. Again, she became nauseated and terribly weak.

After two treatments, Jean's hair fell out and she wore a wig. She liked her wig but felt miserable wearing it during the summer in Texas. It was hot. She missed the feeling of her natural hair blowing in the breeze. Jean really hated it when she went out in public and realized her wig was on crooked!

The vicious cycle continued for six months: get a treatment, become nauseated and weak, slowly regain strength, and go in for another treatment. Jean really didn't like taking her treatments, but knew it was necessary. She was eager to be healthy.

* * * * *

A year later, Jean made a full recovery. She wanted to get back to her "old" life. She and her sister, Dawna, made plans to take a road trip. Jean's hair hadn't yet grown back out, but she felt strong enough to go. She was already daydreaming about the beauty she would see and enjoy.

They decided to travel near San Antonio. Jean had been there before, but Dawna hadn't. The lush greenery and the beautiful running rivers were breathtak-ing. The sisters packed up, told everyone goodbye, and left town. It was exhilarating. Jean felt alive and free again—free from treatments, free from follow-up blood work, free from doctor visits and pharmacy trips. She actually enjoyed food again. Jean thanked God for the life He had given her. She was determined not to sit around being depressed and giving up. She was going to live the life He blessed her with—and live it out loud!

First stop, Gruene, Texas. After leisurely shopping, the sisters dined at the Gristmill Restaurant and sat on the patio. What a pleasure it was to watch the cold Guadalupe River rush within feet of where they sat. Beautiful blue water with whitecaps splashed about as it hit rocks along the way. Dawna couldn't get over the noise of it all. Jean absolutely loved it.

After lunch, they visited the oldest dancehall in the state, the Gruene Hall. That's where many singers and bands have played, including home-grown Willie Nelson and George Strait. Jean knew John Travolta was filmed dancing here in the movie *Michael*, but Dawna didn't.

Second stop, Wimberley, Texas. They packed a lunch and spent all day at Blue Hole. Both thought the spot was one of the prettiest sites in the area. They climbed a short way up the leaning tall cypress trees that grew along the bank. The trees shaded picnic tables and the water. They grabbed the ropes and swung off like Tarzan, eventually plunging into the twenty-foot-deep water-filled blue hole. The crystal-clear water tasted good!

Next stop, New Braunfels, Texas. Jean insisted on spending the day floating down the Comal River. The water temperature is a cool 70 degrees year-round. Jean pitched the wig and put on her rubber swimming cap, just as she did in Wimberley. It looked like one Michael Phelps wore. Trees shaded her cap in Blue Hole, but the trees along the Comal River don't shade the water.

With the sun beating down on Jean's head, the rubber cap quickly got hot. It was burning her scalp. Jean found herself constantly slapping water on top of her head.

Both sisters were excellent swimmers and didn't bother wearing a life jacket. They floated carefree for hours. Eventually, they came to "the chute." Jean had been there before; she knew the danger that could occur if precautions weren't followed. She gave explicit instructions to Dawna. "Whatever you do, hold on to your innertube when you come out of the chute!"

The chute is a water slide at the side of the dam that diverts tubers around the dam so they can continue to float downriver. You travel through the chute swiftly. Dawna understood. They separated so both wouldn't be sucked through the chute at the same time. Dawna went first.

She was all smiles completing the chute and continued happily bobbing downriver.

Then Jean swept through the chute quickly. Oh no! She fell off her innertube.

She frantically tried to grab it but missed. The tube floated on downriver; Jean got sucked under the water. She was slammed onto the river bottom and thrown back into the dam. She was disoriented. She couldn't breathe, she was out of air.

Help! she prayed.

Seeing air bubbles going up, Jean placed both feet on the gravel floor and pushed off with all her might to reach the top. She had to get air—now! Just as her head cleared the water, Jean took a breath and was immediately sucked underwater again and thrown about. She planted her feet as quickly as possible and pushed off as hard as she could again. Jean needed air, she couldn't breathe.

As her head cleared the water, she gasped for air and was yanked under again. She was being hurled about violently. It was a vicious cycle. Jean didn't have the strength to continue fighting for her life much longer. She saw her life flash before her eyes and she was at peace.

The next time she came up for air, a young man yelled, "Are you in trouble?"

Jean quickly inhaled and under she went. As she came up this time, the young man threw her his baby's innertube, and Jean managed to catch it. She went under the water again, but only for a second. That tiny innertube carried her to safety. Jean was relieved. "Thank You, Jesus," she prayed.

Dawna was watching downstream in horror. She was too far away to help. She got out of the water as quickly as possible, ran to Jean, and asked, "What happened? You told me not to lose my innertube. You almost drowned."

"Yeah, I did. I saw my life flash before my eyes," replied Jean. "I saw myself as a baby sitting on a blanket under a tree. I saw myself about four years old with our dog, at age twelve at my party, and driving a truck. That was close. I should have drowned."

They packed up and headed home.

* * * * *

Jean dropped Dawna off at her house and then went straight home. As she began unpacking, Jean couldn't stop thinking about nearly drowning. She began speaking to God out loud. "I'm sorry I never made You Lord of my life. School was more important when I was young. Then Jim was more important. You know I married him. Then absolutely nothing was more important than the birth of little Suzie. She had to be protected and cared for. You are a jealous God, and I've never put You first in my life. You *saved* me when You died for me on the cross. You *saved* my life from cancer. You *saved* my life in New Braunfels. You are my Savior. What have I done for You? If You are my Lord, You must come first. You are worthy of worship and worthy of all praise. From this moment on, Jesus, You are first in my life. Above my family, above my friends, and above my job. I desire to please You. I love You. Amen."*

"You shall have no other gods before me."

Exodus 20:3 NASB

"But seek first the kingdom of God and His righteousness, and all these things shall be added to you."

Matthew 6:33 NKJV

38.

I Can't Tithe, I Have No $

"Sue grew up in church," Memaw began. "She listened to sermons on tithing many times over the years."

"What's a tithe, Memaw?" asked Baby Girl.

"Tithing is when we cheerfully give a small portion of our money back to God. We give it back to Him, because He has given us everything we have," she answered.

Baby Girl replied, "Oh yeah, Mommy taught us that. I know what a tithe is. It's where you take off one zero. Like fifty cents without the zero is five cents, or ten dollars without the zero is one dollar. Mommy taught me and Jo that."

Memaw nodded.

"Well, God is God. He has everything. He doesn't need money. Why does God want my money?" Jo asked.

Memaw continued with the story and didn't answer.

"Sue was now thirty-five years old. She was married and had a little girl named Lynn. Sue was a nurse and her husband worked at a big chemical plant. They made what we call 'good money.' They owned two vehicles, a new house, a four-wheeler, a bay boat, a helicopter and even a six-seater airplane. They loved the outdoors and enjoyed hunting and fishing."

Jo replied, "Memaw, how can you be doing all of that if you are putting God first in your life? They just need to get rid of some of that stuff." Jo was right, they weren't putting God first.

Memaw smiled and continued.

* * * * *

Ms. Crystal was Sue's mother-in-law. She feared God and prayed often. Ms. Crystal loved her family and friends, and they loved her. She's the only person Sue knew that actually heard God speak to her out loud. Some people can't believe that, but Sue certainly did. Ms. Crystal was a godly woman.

One Sunday, Sue went to church with her mother-in-law. Early into the worship service, Ms. Crystal cheerfully placed her tithe into the offering plate and then passed the plate to Sue. Sue just passed it down to the next person. She didn't have extra money to give. Ms. Crystal whispered, "I always give God what is His first, and I've never looked back."

Sue thought about that. She felt convicted.

* * * * *

"I know what that means," said Baby Girl. "It means God is talking to you."

Memaw answered, "Yes, He is."

* * * * *

He let Sue know He wanted her to give. God didn't need her money; He doesn't need our money, or your money Jo. He wanted Sue to trust Him. He wants us to trust Him.

When Sue got home, she sat at her kitchen table with all of her bills and her checkbook. She sat there and told God, "I want to give. I want to be obedient, but I can't. I have this huge stack of bills. See?" A short while later, she said, "All right, God. I'm going to give. I'm going to trust You." She wrote out a $50 check to the church and with excitement couldn't wait to give it.

She continued, "Next month, I'm going to write You a hundred-dollar check. Please help me have more faith in You. I know You don't need my money. You just want my heart, and I want You to have it."

The month after, Sue wrote a check for $150. She was amazed that she still had money left in her account to live on. The following month, she wrote a check for $200. *How is this possible?* she thought. Eventually, Sue was giving a 10 percent tithe on all her and her husband's income.

When Sue realized what God had done, she was in awe. You see, her bills were still the same; they never changed. The income Sue and her husband earned was still the same; it never changed. Sue screamed, "God, that's impossible! Everyone knows if you have the same bills, the same amount of money, you can't spend three hundred dollars more and still have money left over. It's impossible! How awesome are You. Nothing is impossible with You. Oh God, the things You will do if we only believe! I believe. Father God, may I never disappoint You again. Praise God from whom all blessings flow. Hallelujah! Thank You, Jesus."

* * * * *

"You see, guys, people almost think a church is a public building that they shouldn't have to pay for. If it's not paid for, the bank owns it and will resell it to get their money back. If that happened, we wouldn't have our church to worship in. Tithes pay for the church. On top of that, tithes pay the electric bill, the water bill, the coffee served before Sunday school, the secretary's salary, the pastor's salary, the music director's salary, the youth minister's salary, the broken refrigerator, the leaking toilet… Get the idea? We don't have a big congregation, so the money coming in to pay bills at our church is limited. Thankfully, we have church members that enjoy going to God's house to work. They don't get paid; they volunteer. They do it because they love God and they want to take care of His house."

"Is that why you go in on Wednesdays, to help out in the choir or the library, Memaw?"

"Yes, it is. When I go, I get to tend to my Father's House. It makes me happy. I pray as I file papers or organize books. I love it! Some play the piano, others sing. Some cut grass, others paint or clean or make repairs. We all have something we can offer.

"The church is not a country club that we go to for people to entertain us or serve us; we go to serve others. We are supposed to make others comfortable and feel accepted. One day I won't be able to do a lot physically for God's house, but until that day is here, I will."

Jo responded, "When I get big, Memaw, I'm going to work at God's house, too."

"Me too," answered Baby Girl.*

"Will a man rob God? Yet you are robbing Me! But you say, 'How have we robbed You?' In tithes and offerings."

Malachi 3:8 NASB

...for God loves a cheerful giver.

2 Corinthians 9:7 NIV

"They all gave out of their wealth; but she, out of her poverty, put in everything-all she had to live on."

Mark 12:44 NIV

39.

Two Very Different Families

Meet the Jacksons. Roy Jackson is a very shy eight-year-old little boy. If you ask him a question, he nods yes or no and speaks only if he has to. Lisa is Roy's little sister; she is anything but shy. Lisa talks to everybody, no matter what. She's loud and bubbly and never shuts up. Roy's parents think it's cute, but Roy thinks it's annoying.

It's summertime. The Jacksons are extremely poor. They lost their home one week ago and are now living in the woods. Their so-called house consists of a piece of plywood lodged between two trees. They stay under it when it gets too hot or when it rains. The family walks to the gas station to use the bathroom and wash their hands.

Mr. Jackson had been out of work for a while. He recently started a job cutting down trees. Roy's dad is a big, proud, strong man who has never asked anyone for help and says he never will.

Mrs. Jackson is a homemaker. She loves taking care of her family. She's humble and full of faith. Roy's mom talks to God all the time. She told the kids they were on a camping trip. She tried hard to make it seem as though all was normal.

* * * * *

One day, a boy named Jack was walking down a dirt road and came upon Roy. Jack stuck his hand out and said, "Hello, my name is Jack. What's your name?" Roy was so shy, he barely looked up to see who was talking to him. Jack then repeated his question with his hand still outstretched.

Roy glanced up at Jack and asked, "Who, me? I'm Roy," and shook Jack's hand.

"Nice to meet you Roy. You live around here?" Jack asked.

Lisa came running up to the boys. She heard everything, "Hi, I'm Lisa. Roy's shy. He doesn't talk much. We're camping right over there. Come see. Where do you live? Why are you here? What are you doing today? Do you want to play hide and seek in the woods with us?" Lisa grabbed Jack's hand and dragged him into the woods. She told him, "We stay here. Mom! Come meet my very best new friend, Jack."

Mom smiled and shook Jack's hand. "I'm Mrs. Gertrude Jackson. Nice to meet you."

"And you," said Jack.

She asked, "Would you like to stay for supper?"

Roy thought, *No, no, please don't stay.* Jack said, "I'd love to."

The Jacksons had been eating homemade soup since they fell on hard times, but things were going to get better soon since Mr. Jackson went back to work. He just got in and parked his old beat-up truck off the road. When Jack saw him, he was shocked at how big and tall Mr. Jackson was.

Roy's mom came out with a pot of soup. "Hi, honey, meet Jack. Jack, this is Mr. Jackson. Jack is staying for supper."

Mr. Jackson wasn't happy. How could she invite someone to eat with them? They didn't have enough food for themselves.

Jack held out his hand to shake Mr. Jackson's hand. Mr. Jackson reluctantly shook Jack's hand. Mom poured out ¾ of a bowl of soup for Jack, ½ cup soup for Roy and for Lisa, and a full bowl for Mr. Jackson. Mr. Jackson got the most because he had to have his strength to cut down trees.

Jack saw that Mrs. Jackson had hardly any soup at all. He thought, *These people are poor and hungry.*

Lisa talked all during supper. Jack couldn't get over the fact that Mrs. Jackson gave up her food and did without for him, a guest. Now that's showing true love for your neighbor. She didn't know Jack, yet she did without and fed him. He thinks Mrs. Jackson may be the sweetest woman he's ever met. Jack ate about half of his bowl of soup.

Jack said the soup was delicious and he had no room in his belly to take another bite. "Thank you so much, Mr. and Mrs. Jackson. Your kindness is greatly appreciated. I have to really be getting home now. But before I go, would it be all right if Roy and Lisa came to my house tomorrow afternoon and stay for supper? I'd like to show them the town since y'all are new here."

All Roy could hope for is that they would say no. *Just say no,* he thought.

"Sure, Jack. That is mighty sweet of you," answered Mrs. Jackson.

Jack replied, "I'll be here tomorrow at two o'clock, if that's OK?"

"That will be fine," she answered. Jack went home.

Jack was concerned for his new friends. He told his mom all about them. Mrs. Rogers told Jack she was thrilled he invited them over. She was planning a huge dinner and named off mac and cheese, chicken nuggets, French fries, hamburgers… Jack stopped her. He told her that should be plenty. Mrs. Rogers wanted to have plenty of food, after all, that Lisa sounded mighty energetic.

Jack couldn't wait to tell his dad about the Jacksons, and that Roy and Lisa would be over tomorrow for a visit.

"That's fine, Son. Isn't that the poor family that lives on the out skirt of town?" asked Jack's dad.

"Yes, Dad. Roy and Lisa are my friends. I like them. They invited me to supper and I ate with them. They have so little, Dad. Surely, we can help them some way. Mom is planning a feast for a king. I had soup, mostly water with a little bit of corn in it. My heart broke."

"I'm proud of you. Under the circumstances, some folks might treat them less than human," his dad replied.

"I know, Dad. I just try to think how Jesus wants me to treat people. They were so kind to me."

Mr. Rogers thought a lot about all he had just learned.

* * * * *

Roy sure hoped Jack wouldn't show up today at two o'clock. It was one minute before 2:00 p.m. Roy was relieved Jack hadn't come.

Suddenly, Julie started hollering and running out to the road. "Jack, Jack, you're here. You came. Momma we have to go see the town. We'll be back later."

Roy followed Lisa.

Lisa grabbed Jack's hand. "You came, Jack, you came. I'm so glad you came. I'm excited to go to your house. Do we get to meet your mom and dad? Are we going to eat at your house? Can I—"

Roy jumped in, "Hi, Jack."

The kids walked straight to Jack's house. Roy couldn't believe it. They were in awe. It wasn't too big, but it was beautiful. Mrs. Rogers ran out of the house to meet them. You would have thought Lisa was her little girl. Lisa ran up to her, they hugged so long and swayed left and right.

Mrs. Rogers said, "I've been waiting for you. I cooked a special meal for you and Roy. I hope you like it. I'm Mrs. Rogers. Mr. Rogers will be home soon. You are a mighty pretty little girl, Lisa."

Mrs. Rogers turned her attention to Roy. She liked him just as soon as she saw those beautiful big brown eyes. *How sweet,* she thought.

Roy did manage to say, "Nice to meet you."

Lisa and Jack were surprised he actually spoke.

Mr. Rogers drove up and got out of the car wearing a suit with a tie and carrying his brief case. He sure looked a lot different than Roy's dad. Roy was a bit nervous, but after Mr. Rogers talked to him, you would have thought Roy had known him all his life.

"Let's go eat while the food is hot," said Mrs. Rogers.

They all ran into the house and went straight through to the kitchen. There was fried chicken, mashed potatoes, peas, fried okra, hamburgers, pie, and more. Lisa said, "Wow. That's my favorite."

Everybody washed their hands and sat at the table. Lisa reached for the mac and cheese, then she looked at Jack. Jack had his head down ready to pray. Lisa and Roy bowed their heads. Mr. Rogers said grace and thanked God for Roy and Lisa. Roy and Lisa really listened to each word of the blessing.

Everyone began passing around bowls of food and getting what they wanted. Lisa got too much. She couldn't eat everything on her plate. Roy served himself little by little; he didn't waste any food. Lisa and Roy ate until they were stuffed.

After the meal, Mrs. Rogers began cleaning the kitchen. Roy took his new friends upstairs to check out his bedroom, and then outside to play.

* * * * *

Meanwhile, Roy's mom and dad were at their makeshift home. Mrs. Jackson prayed all the time, especially for her family. She was sad about the hard times they fell on, but praised God for Mr. Jackson's new job. Roy's dad used to pray a lot, but not anymore. Before things fell apart, Mr. Jackson was proud of the fact that his family lived well. He was also proud

of the fact that he had $453,096.42 in the bank. The Jackson family was well off. Mr. Jackson believed that only happened because of his hard work over the years. But overnight, everything came crashing down.

Mr. Jackson was mad at God. He blamed God for losing his job earlier. He blamed God for allowing a thief to hack into his bank account and steal all his money. He blamed God that he couldn't pay for his apartment and couldn't feed his family well. Good people had offered to help him, but he always refused. Proud Mr. Jackson wasn't proud anymore. Mr. Jackson was angry; he refused to talk to God about anything!

The kids were having a wonderful time. Roy couldn't believe he got along so well with Jack and Lisa. He thanked God for his new friends. Lisa told Jack that he was her brother. Jack felt special. They all played hard and had gotten dirty. Jack's mom let Lisa and Roy to take a shower and gave them clean clothes to wear. She even gave them two bags of Jack's old clothes he couldn't wear anymore to take home.

On their way out, Mrs. Rogers even handed them two bags of leftovers. She said, "Y'all will be doing me a huge favor if you take this home. I cooked too much food and I'd like you to have it."

Lisa was all smiles. "Sure, Mrs. Rogers, we'll take it. Thank you."

When they got home, Lisa told her mom all about the fun they had with Jack and his parents. Mrs. Jackson was thankful for the leftovers and the clothes and glad the kids took a shower. She prayed silently, *Thank You for providing. Thank You for the food and clothing. Thank You for Jack and his family.*

Thank You for Your blessings.

Suddenly, Roy's dad wasn't mad at God anymore. He could see that God was providing for them. He prayed for the very first time in a very long time. "Forgive me, Father, for turning away from You. Please help me provide for my family. They deserve better. My money used to be my god, but not anymore. I am no longer proud. I am dependent on You. You are my God. Help me keep my eyes focused on You and not on my circumstances. Amen."

* * * * *

The next day, Jack's dad came home from work exhausted. He explained that things were hectic because two men walked off the job. He didn't know how they would catch up.

Jack pleaded, "Dad, you've got to go meet Mr. Jackson. Maybe he will be interested in a job. He's a big strong man."

"Get my keys, Son, and let's head over there," his dad replied.

Jack and his dad parked behind Mr. Jackson's truck. Jack introduced his dad to Mr. and Mrs. Jackson.

Lisa came running up. "Hi, Jack. Hi, Mr. Rogers. How are you? Glad to see you. Meet my parents, Mom and Dad."

Mr. Rogers smiled. Lisa was the cutest thing ever.

Mr. Rogers asked Mr. Jackson if he could speak to him privately. They walked out to his truck and talked.

The kids started playing chase. Mrs. Jackson wondered what in the world was going on.

"Mr. Jackson, sir, I have a real problem. I could use your help," said Mr. Rogers.

Mr. Jackson thought, *Lord, please let him offer me a better job.*

"You see, I had two men quit working for my company today. We have so much work lined up. I need to hire two men. It's hard physical labor, but it pays well. Are you interested?"

"You bet. When can I start?" Roy's dad asked.

Mr. Rogers answered, "Tomorrow at seven a.m. I tell you what, if you can do the work of two men, I'll pay you double. See you tomorrow."

They shook hands. Boy, was Mr. Jackson thrilled. *A real job with good pay.* Now, he will be able to take good care of his family. *Thank You, Lord.*

Roy's dad was strong and easily did the work of three men. He was thankful for the job. Roy's dad thought, *I never should have turned away from God. I'm glad He's my best friend again.* Mr. Jackson is no longer angry, he's happy. He talks to God every day.

* * * * *

Weeks later, the Jacksons moved into a house on the same street where Jack lives. It was great visiting on the weekends. The Jacksons and the Rogers became very close friends. Mr. Jackson praised God for providing for him and his family. He thought, *We are two very different families, but we are both really the same. You are our Father. We are all Your children. We are all loved by You, the Almighty, the Alpha and the Omega.* (That's the beginning and the end.) *Thank You, Lord, for saving me. I thank You for all You've ever done for us and for all that You are about to do. Amen.*

Pride goes before destruction, and a haughty spirit before stumbling. It is better to be humble in spirit with the lowly than to divide the spoil with the proud.

Proverbs 16:18–19 NASB

But He gives a greater grace. Therefore it says: "God is opposed to the proud, but gives grace to the humble."

James 4:6 NASB

40.

Cassie Is Courageous

Becky invited three of her friends over this Friday to stay the night. Ms. Gena, Becky's mom, had it all planned out. She was going to cook hamburgers and hot dogs. She already had brownies made and snacks in the pantry. Becky was excited.

Becky recently read a book about a group of girls on vacation. At one point in the story, the girls held a séance. The story intrigued Becky. She thought it would be neat to hold a séance with her friends. She wanted to talk to her grandmother. Grams had passed two years ago and Becky missed her. She also planned on staying up late and watching movies all night.

When Emily, Diane and Cassie arrived, they placed their belongings in Becky's room. Shortly thereafter, they went downstairs and ate supper. Ms. Gena enjoyed spending time with the girls. She loved watching them munch out.

Afterward, the girls went outside and hung out until dark. When the mosquitoes began to swarm, the girls ran inside and up to Becky's room. They played music on the radio. A pillow fight broke out. The girls were running and yelling and acting crazy. Becky's mom came upstairs and swung open the door. "What's going on? You all know better!" Everyone stopped dead in their tracks. Mrs. Gena then turned and left the room.

The girls giggled quietly. Becky whispered, "Let's hold a séance." Two girls said yeah, but Cassie didn't like the sound of it. "What is a séance?" one asked. Becky explained, "It's where we hold hands and call up someone who has already passed. I want to talk to Grammy. She passed two years ago." They all sat on the floor in a circle and grabbed hands.

Before Becky could say a word, Cassie said, "No! We can't do this. Your grandma is in heaven. She's with Jesus. She can't talk to you right now."

Becky asked, "What do you mean, Cassie?"

"I mean the Bible tells us not to conjure up spirits. You might get an answer, but it wouldn't be from God. This is the devil's world. If you do this, he might answer. Remember, we studied this. King Saul went to a sorcerer. That's like a witch. He winds up dying because he was unfaithful to God. The Bible says a lot more about witchcraft and stuff, but that I clearly remember."

Becky felt awful. She told the girls she thought it would just be a fun thing to do. She asked Cassie not to go home. Becky called her mom upstairs and told her what happened. Ms. Gena was glad

they called her. She grabbed her Bible, and they had Bible study right then.

Mrs. Gena explained, "Satan reigns on this earth. That's why it is ugly and full of sin. The Bible says he roams the earth to see who he can devour. To eat up." The girls had no idea. Not until we get to heaven will it be glorious and free of sin.

"The devil has power, but it is evil power. He can give you power, and money, and other things; but he's not being nice to you. He wants to turn you away from Jesus." Ms. Gena continued, "Leviticus 19:31 [NASB] reads, 'Do not turn to mediums or spiritists; do not seek them out to be defiled by them. I am the LORD your God.'"

Everyone learned that contacting spirits goes against God's Word.

"Thanks, Mom. I'll talk to Grams when I get to heaven," said Becky.

"Good," said Cassie.

Becky reached for the Yahtzee game and said, "Who wants to play?"

Emily answered, "No one. Let's dance."

41.

Charlie's So Funny

Everyone in town knew Charlie. He wore the same clothes nearly every day. He was always smiling and happy. When he walked down the street, he would sometimes dance a bit. Many times, Charlie sang. He loved children. As Charlie came upon children, he would have to stop and talk to them. He did things to make them laugh. All the kids loved Mr. Charlie.

But not their parents. No, they tried to avoid Mr. Charlie. If they saw him coming down the street, most would walk to the other side of the street. Parents didn't want to talk to Mr. Charlie. They could tell by the way Mr. Charlie walked that he was drunk. They could smell liquor on his breath. Sometimes, Mr. Charlie would just stumble to the ground. Kids thought he was playing. They would run right up to him and talk and laugh with him. Easton's dad helped Mr. Charlie get up one time. *Boy, Mr. Charlie smells terrible and could use a bath,* he thought.

Charlie lives with unimaginable guilt. When Charlie was nineteen, he lost his dad in a car wreck. Charlie was driving. He relives that terrible scene in his head, over and over again almost daily. It didn't matter to Charlie that the accident wasn't his fault; he still couldn't shake the guilt.

When Charlie drinks and gets drunk, he doesn't think about the accident. Charlie drinks every day.

* * * * *

This particular night, Drunk Charlie was laying on a bench at the playground. He was all alone. At three o'clock in the morning, Charlie was awake and gazing at the stars. He began to think, *How did those starts get there? Who made the stars? For that matter, who made the trees, the planets and the animals?* Charlie realized that there had to be a Creator to create such beauty. He remembered his mom and grandma occasionally mentioning God or Jesus, but Charlie never listened.

At that very moment, God opened Charlie's heart. Charlie instantly knew God created all things. Charlie knew he was a sinner. He knew he needed saving. Charlie rolled off that bench to his knees quickly. He passionately prayed, "Dear Jesus, I'm a sinner. I've pretty much ruined my life and I'm sorry. Please forgive me of all my sins. Come live in my heart. Help me to stop drinking and take away my guilt. Thank You, Jesus. Thank You. You've set me free. I'm not Drunk Charlie anymore. I'm a new creation. Help me live for You all the days of my life. I love You. Amen." Charlie got up and went home.

Charlie took a shower. He put on clean clothes. Charlie cleaned his house and his yard. Afterward, he showered again and got dressed to walk to town. Charlie looked like he was going to Sunday school. He smelled nice, his clothes were wrinkle-free, and his hair was combed.

Charlie first went to the barber and got a haircut. He then walked to the grocery store and bought groceries. When kids ran up to him, he smiled and politely said good morning.

The parents were taken aback. *Is that truly Drunk Charlie? I don't believe it. It can't be Drunk Charlie! He's changed. He's really changed. He's not the same man.* They spoke kindly to Mr. Charlie

and shook his hand to introduce themselves to him. Mr. Charlie was all smiles.

* * * * *

That Sunday, Mr. Charlie walked into his local church for the first time. Boy, it was beautiful! All the people were so nice. They greeted him and told him they were so glad he was there. Mr. Charlie was thinking on the inside, *You have no idea how glad I am to be here.* He was thrilled to be in God's house—his Father's house! Mr. Charlie was loved, and he has a home in heaven. He imagined his dad in the arms of Jesus and was overjoyed.

Mr. Charlie had changed. God made him a new creation and everyone could see it. Charlie learned as much as he could about the Bible. In time, he began teaching a Sunday school class. A lot of people loved his class because he was so real. Charlie told them how bad a sinner he was and how he almost let guilt ruin his life. Then he told them about Jesus. What Jesus had done for him. What Jesus will do for anyone that trust in Him. He said, "I'm clean, white-as-snow clean, through Jesus. There's tremendous power in that name, the mighty name of Jesus. I'm living proof!"

Though your sins be as scarlet, they shall be as white as snow; though they be red like crimson, they shall be as wool.

Isaiah 1:18 KJV

"So if the Son sets you free, you will be free indeed."

John 8:36 NIV

42.

Mrs. Lulu

Mrs. Lulu loved nothing more than seeing smiles on children's faces as they raced upstairs to her Sunday school classroom. The kids were loud and inattentive at times, even rebellious, but she loved them all the same.

Chloe was eight years old. She was different from the others. She followed directions and wasn't disruptive. Chloe was quiet and very polite. She really focused on Mrs. Lulu during class. Mrs. Lulu had a way of asking a question that helped the children easily figure out the answer. When she raised a question during the lesson, most of the little children sitting on the floor would bounce up and down and stretch their hands as high as possible. Each desperately wanted to be chosen to answer. Each, that is, except Chloe.

No matter how hard Mrs. Lulu tried, she couldn't get Chloe to engage. Chloe kept silent. This was Chloe's second year with Mrs. Lulu. Mrs. Lulu thought, *Am I getting through to her? Is she learning anything about Jesus?* "These children need You, Lord. Please help me instill in them their need for You in their life. I want them to know You are their heavenly Father, Abba Father. Help me give them Jesus, the light of the world," she prayed.

Mrs. Lulu spent hours during the week preparing to teach Sunday school. She called it a labor of love. She was creative in devising crafts for the children to put together. The kids loved to paint, draw, play games, use glitter, cut out paper objects, and put puzzles together. All in all, it was usually quite a mess to clean up afterward. Though Chloe barely spoke, she always had her craft put together the quickest and with the least mess. That pleased Mrs. Lulu.

In the fall of this year, Chloe's Sunday school class was promoted to Mrs. Felicia's class. Mrs. Lulu loved getting her new students for the year, but she did miss those that moved on. She prayed for all her students for years, regardless of their age. Chloe was always in the back of her mind.

* * * * *

Mrs. Lulu invested hundreds of hours preparing and teaching her students the Bible. At times, she pondered whether her efforts truly made any difference. Regardless, Mrs. Lulu knew God had called her to teach Sunday school, just as He called her to teach public school. To repeat instructions over and over, would drive many adults crazy, but not Mrs. Lulu.

She mastered the ability to keep children focused and on task.

* * * * *

Years rolled by. Chloe and her family went on vacation to Kentucky. While there, her parents took them to Crystal Onyx Cave. Chloe was mesmerized. The cave was like nothing she had ever seen. Seemed like it was something from another planet. The formations inside were magnificent. Chloe thought it was beautiful.

The lady that gave the tour truly loved God's creation and wanted others to enjoy it as well. It was 94 degrees outside the cave, but once they descended a few feet inside, the temperature was a cool 60 degrees. The group walked in single file, winding around and hiking up and down as they followed the guide. The information their guide fed them during the tour was much too much to comprehend so quickly.

Deep within the cave, all the hikers were instructed to sit on benches. The guide warned, "The lights will be turned off." Then the lights were turned off. It was black.

No one there had ever experienced pitch-black darkness like this before. Chloe couldn't see her hand two inches from her nose. Unbelievable. She knew if she could light a little candle, the whole cave would have been lit up. The tour guide then had the lights turned back on and everyone hiked back outside.

On their way back to their cabin, Chloe couldn't stop thinking about the black darkness inside the cave. *There's darkness. Then there's pitch-black darkness. There's light. And then there's bright, radiant light, and His name is Jesus. Jesus is the light of the world.* "Jesus is the light! He is the light of the world!" she exclaimed. "Jesus lives in me. That's what Mrs. Lulu was trying to teach me. If I let Jesus shine, then I can light up the whole world!"

Her mom and dad were delighted.

There doesn't have to be a million kids with a million little candles to light up the world. There can be just one kid that opens their heart and lets Jesus shine. That can be me. I have that power. I can let Jesus light up the whole world! It's my choice. Do I let Jesus shine? Yes!

In church the following week, Chloe sang to Jesus. She hoped to be picked to answer every question in Sunday school. Chloe never stopped talking about the precious name of Jesus.

Mrs. Lulu couldn't have been more thrilled.

"You are the light of the world. A town built on a hill cannot be hidden."

Matthew 5:14 NIV

When Jesus spoke again to the people, he said, "I am the light of the world. Whoever follows me will never walk in darkness, but will have the light of life."

John 8:12 NIV

43.

Omnipotent (All-Powerful) God

This is a story about Little Levi and his sister, Abby. Their grandma is talking to them about God. She wants them to know how important God is and why we are to obey him.

Grandma begins, "Can you tell me something special about God? And, can you tell me what it means when we say God is a jealous God?"

Levi and Abby begin shouting, "He's supposed to be first in our lives! He's always with us! He never leaves us! He knows what we're thinking! He hears our prayers and answers our prayers, just like He did for Joshua and everybody else in the Bible! He loves us more than anyone! Jesus died for me! He saved us!"

Grandma was pleased. "When God speaks, it's important. God doesn't say one thing and mean something else. He isn't joking. His Word is Truth. That's why we can depend on Him. His promises are never broken."

Little Levi answered, "Like when Abraham took Isaac up to sacrifice him. Abraham did exactly what God told him to do because he knew God meant business. But then God told him to stop, and Abraham stopped."

Abby is sitting still and taking it all in.

"God rewarded Abraham, didn't he, Grandma?" asked Levi.

"Oh yes, he did. God blessed Abraham in a mighty way. We are all sons of Abraham," she answered. "Thousands of years ago, the Jews were slaves in Egypt under Pharaoh. A pharaoh is like a king. He rules the land. He forced God's children to make bricks by stomping mud and straw together with their feet. God instructed Moses to go to Pharaoh and say, 'Let my people go, so they may worship me.' Moses went to Pharaoh and told him to let God's children go, but Pharaoh said no. Because Pharaoh was stubborn and continued to refuse to let God's children go, God cast plagues upon the land. Can you name the first plague?"

Levi and Abby shouted, "The water turned into blood. No, it was the frogs. I think it was the locusts. Also, the people got bad sores."

Grandma admitted that the water turned to blood was the first plague. "No one could drink water for seven days. It smelled awful. Later, God sent Moses back to Pharaoh. Moses repeated God's command, "Let my people go," but again Pharaoh refused. God punished Egypt this time with a plague of frogs. Millions of frogs everywhere. Frogs were in their beds, in their food, on the ceilings and on the floors. No one could get rid of them. The third time Pharaoh refused to let the Israelites leave, God sent a plague of lice. The lice were in their hair and all over their bodies; and they bite! The bites weren't really painful, but they were very annoying. The poor animals had lice, too."

Little Levi said, "Yeah, but God protected His children and they didn't suffer like the bad Egyptians did."

Grandma said, "Oh no, dear. The Israelites did suffer. These three plagues affected everyone in Egypt, Israelites and Egyptians."

* * * * *

Moses went to Pharaoh for the fourth time and said, "Let my people go," but Pharaoh still said no! God sent the fourth plague of flies upon Pharaoh and the Egyptians, but He protected his children this time. Flies were in the Egyptians food, beds, hair, ears, and up their noses. Flies covered the animal's eyes and noses and mouths, too. It was awful. The Egyptians prayed to their idols to stop the plague of flies. Idols have no power!

Only the Egyptians were affected by the plagues God cast upon them from here on out. God continued to protect his children. The fifth plague was the death of the animals in the fields. The sixth plague was painful sores covering people and animals. The seventh plague was fire and hail falling from the sky that killed everything not protected by shelter. Swarms of locusts that devoured all their plants was the eighth plague, and the ninth plague was three days and three nights of pitch-black darkness. All these terrible things happened because Pharaoh refused to obey God and let His people go. The Israelites were thankful God protected them from these torments.

The tenth and final plague cast on Egypt was the death of the firstborn and the firstborn of the animals. God's children were protected as long as they obeyed God. They were to smear the blood of a sacrificed lamb on their doorposts. When God saw the blood on their doorpost, He passed over their house and did not harm them as he punished the Egyptians. This was called Passover. All of the Egyptian's firstborn sons died, including Pharaoh's son. Afterward, Pharaoh told Moses to take his people and leave Egypt.

God delivered the Israelites out of Egypt. Moses led God's children through the parted waters of the Red Sea, and they walked across on dry land, not mud.

When Jesus was a little boy, He celebrated Passover with his mom and dad, Mary and Joseph. They celebrated freedom from slavery and oppression. Passover is still celebrated. As Christians, we celebrate Passover because we are free from sin and death. When our life is finished here on earth, Jesus takes us home with Him. We never die.

* * * * *

Grandma asked, "What would have happened if the Israelites didn't mark their houses with lamb's blood? What if they thought God was just joking?"

Little Levi answered, "The firstborn kid would die, because God said to do it, and they didn't listen."

Grandma nodded.

"Grandma, we want to go to church. Mommy says no one can go to church. God can protect us like He did the Israelites. Why can't we go?" asked Levi. "We're tired of staying home."

"A terrible disease is sweeping through our land. We have never experienced anything like it. It started in one country, and within days, has streaked around the entire world. It's devastating. People are getting sick and unfortunately, many are dying. People are scared."

Levi said he wasn't scared of getting sick. He said, "God comes first. Nobody can stop us from going to church."

Abby said, "Yeah, Grandma, I really want to see Ms. Sharon in Sunday school."

Levi continued, "God won't let us get sick if we are there for Him."

Grandma explained, "We can't go to church right now because of the mandate: social distancing. We stay at home as much as possible so we don't spread the disease to others. We are protecting elderly and unhealthy people who may not be able to fight it.

"Lepers in Biblical times couldn't live near healthy people. They had to cry out, 'Unclean' if anyone should approach. It was sad, but they didn't want to spread the disease. They followed orders to protect other people.

"Remember when the disciples asked Jesus if they had to pay taxes, give their money to Rome? They thought the law was unfair. We are to give God our hearts. Jesus taught the disciples to give Caesar the things that are Caesar's. They were to follow the law just as we are to follow the law.

"We can still worship together. We can use our computer, cell phone or TV. We don't stop singing praises or worshiping God just because we can't go to church. We do it at home, inside, just like the Israelites did during Passover. Hopefully, we worship God every day of the week and not just on Sundays in church.

"Jesus' light still shines in times like these. I think it shines brighter. More people are turning to God in their distress. The devil wants us to cry and worry and feel awful, but we know God is in control. He is all-knowing, all-powerful and always with us. God instructs us to live without fear and without worry. We get to live with joy—the joy only Jesus can give. It's a privilege to gather and worship with others, and we will go to church as soon as we are allowed to."

Abby said, "Let's sing 'This Little of Light of Mine.'"

Everyone broke out in song while making the hand motions. They sang it a couple of times and were happy and loud!

The grass withers, the flower fades, but the word of our God stands forever.

Isaiah 40:8 NASB

"BEHOLD, THE VIRGIN SHALL BE WITH CHILD AND SHALL BEAR A SON, AND THEY SHALL CALL HIS NAME IMMANUEL," which translated means, "GOD WITH US."

Matthew 1:23 NASB

Jesus Christ is the same yesterday and today and forever.

Hebrews 13:8 NASB

44.

Devil, You Can't Stop ME!

For years, Nancy attended church. She delighted in knowing God's love for her was immeasurable. She talked to God about everything. She was thankful for green grass and the green trees. She thanked God for blue skies and white clouds. She thanked Him for the springtime, summertime, winter and fall. Nancy found God's creation magnificent. She especially prayed for her family and for the salvation of every lost soul. Nancy didn't like to think about the devil. She knew he was evil.

Nancy's entire life seemed to be smooth sailing. She was happy. There were a few headaches along the way, but nothing serious. She thought of how King David wore a priestly outfit and danced before the Lord with all his might as he and the Israelites brought up the Ark of the Lord. They shouted with joy and blew ram's horns like a trumpet. When David's wife, Michal, saw him dancing, she despised him. Why would anyone despise someone for being happy and dancing before the Lord? she wondered.

Nancy listened to godly music as she worked. At times, she danced and sang before God. Knowing Jesus was right there with her, she imagined Him holding her hand and spinning her around. It was a great feeling, and she couldn't help but laugh and sing all the louder. In the midst of overwhelming joy, suddenly she was given devastating news. Her heart ached. Those she cared for were in trouble. She hated how the devil tormented them. With tears flowing, she prayed and asked God to take care of them.

As Nancy did the Lord's work and kept her eyes focused on Him, she was at peace. The moment she stopped focusing on God and focused on the circumstances surrounding her friends, she felt a sense of doom. Quickly, she chose to call upon God and He comforted her.

* * * * *

On Wednesdays, Nancy liked to organize the church library. While checking in books, she was overcome with a sense of dread. The Bible says, "Do not fear," but Nancy couldn't shake the terrible feeling. She felt like she was going to jump out of her skin.

Two deacons were working on toilets upstairs. Nancy needed to pray with someone right then. "Where two or more are gathered in His name, He is there," she recalled. She ran up those stairs and found the men coming out of the bathroom carrying plumbing materials. Laughing, they offered Nancy something dirty to carry, but she declined.

Just as they reached the stairs, Nancy interrupted the pleasantries. "We have to pray. We have to pray right now," she said with urgency in her voice. Harry and Raymond stopped dead in their track. "What's wrong?" Harry asked. Nancy shared what was eating at her. Knowing Jesus stood in the center of them, the three grabbed hands and prayed. Raymond led the prayer, Nancy prayed, and Harry closed in prayer. Nancy immediately felt at peace.

* * * * *

Four days later, Nancy's Sunday school teacher became ill and couldn't teach that morning. Nancy wasn't a teacher, but she volunteered to head the class. Out of the blue, a woman stood up. She was angry. She asked Nancy a question and

demanded an answer. The woman was loud and pointed her finger at Nancy. Nancy was confused. What's going on? Nancy couldn't remember what the question was because she was shocked at the woman's behavior.

Nancy silently prayed, *Give me Your words, Father.*

Finally, Nancy said, "All I can say is, if we keep our eyes focused on God"— she pointed upward—"then all of this will take care of itself." She circled her hands around the room.

The woman became calm, apologized and sat down. The study concluded in prayer.

After church, Nancy went home. She realized that suddenly bad things were happening every few days.

After eating lunch and taking a nap, Nancy began typing up godly stories she had told her family in the past. While praying, God told her to combine the stories and publish a storybook.

Nancy couldn't type fast enough. She was excited that God chose her for this job. Nancy was thrilled.

After the sermon Sunday, Pastor invited Nancy to the pulpit to share with the church how God was using her in a mighty way to glorify Him. Nancy excitedly told the church all that God was leading her to do. She explained that though she knew nothing about publishing a book or using a computer, she knew God did, and He would see her through.

Afterward, a dear couple from the congregation approached her. They told her that God is doing something awesome. "Stay in prayer. You know the devil is going to hate this. He doesn't want you or God to succeed." Nancy thought, *God fights my battles and He always wins. No problem, right?*

Nancy immersed herself in typing up the stories God had given her over the years. She rejoiced in His love. WHAM! Nancy received the meanest phone call ever. It was ugly and couldn't have been any worse. Nancy stayed up all night and prayed. She asked God for forgiveness and cried out, "I am to be still. You are my fortress; I will not be shaken. You fight my battles." She realized the devil wanted her to focus on her problems and not on God. Nancy was thankful for God's amazing grace. She was determined to please Him. Nancy chose to dance and she sang before the Lord!

After making amends the next morning, Nancy told God, "The devil wants me to give up and cry and be sad. I have cried and I am sad about all of these problems, but I'm overjoyed to know this job is of You. You chose me. I can do this only through You. You will fight for me. When the devil interferes, I will pray, 'Jesus, Jesus, Jesus, help me.'"

Nancy sang "Run Devil Run" by David Crowder. She loved the catchy tune and jazzy beat. The words reminded her of Who fights for us. When the devil tries to take a shot at us, "he has none, but we have God. We have Jesus Christ. We have the Holy Ghost! He continues and says we have the power to make the devil be gone.

Nancy felt sorry for unsaved people. Who do they go to when they are hurting? Our battles belong to the Lord, and without Jesus, we lose. Nancy had a choice to make. She chose to trust God. Hallelujah!*

"I call upon the LORD, who is worthy to be praised, and I am saved from my enemies."

2 Samuel 22:4 NASB

Oh give thanks to the LORD, call upon His name; make known His deeds among the peoples.

1 Chronicles 16:8 NASB

About the Author

JoAnn Vicknair is an ordinary grandmother. She will tell you she had no creative mind, that is, until God answered her prayer. And she never planned on publishing a book, until God told her to.

Years ago, JoAnn found herself unable to tell her grandchildren a decent story when they asked for one. She routinely prayed, "God, give me stories of You. They need You in their lives. Help them to know You and draw closer to You." God answered her prayers.

Shortly thereafter, JoAnn began journaling the stories she told. The journal began falling apart. Only recently did she decide to print them. During prayer, as she typed, God told her to combine the stories and have them published. JoAnn was moved. She had no idea what that would entail, but she trusted God did.